# TRAIN WRECKED

Before the gunmen could move, Fargo bent down, drawing his Arkansas toothpick. He twisted at the waist and flung the knife at the closest outlaw. The knife sunk to the hilt in the man's heart. He slumped to his knees, still holding onto the shotgun, and there was a deafening thunderclap as he shot a hole in the floor of the train car. Pandemonium erupted. Women screamed, men cursed, and everyone was moving.

Fargo whirled in the direction of the other outlaw, throwing himself to the floor, reaching for his Colt, grasping the handle with a finger around the trigger. But the outlaw was already drawing a bead on Fargo right between the eyes, and there was no time to pull his pistol up.

He was a dead man . . . .

# THE TRAILSMAN

#243

# WEST TEXAS UPRISING

by

Jon Sharpe

A SIGNET BOOK

SIGNET
Published by New American Library, a division of
Penguin Putnam Inc., 375 Hudson Street,
New York, New York 10014, U.S.A.
Penguin Books Ltd, 10 Strand,
London WC2R ORL, England
Penguin Books Australia Ltd, Ringwood,
Victoria, Australia
Penguin Books Canada Ltd, 10 Alcorn Avenue,
Toronto, Ontario, Canada M4V 3B2
Penguin Books (N.Z.) Ltd, 182–190 Wairau Road,
Auckland 10, New Zealand

Penguin Books Ltd, Registered Offices:
Harmondsworth, Middlesex, England

First published by Signet, an imprint of New American Library,
a division of Penguin Putnam Inc.

First Printing, January 2002
10  9  8  7  6  5  4  3  2  1

The first chapter of this title originally appeared in *Wyoming Whirlwind*,
the two hundred forty-second volume in this series.

# The Trailsman

Beginnings . . . they bend the tree and they mark the man. Skye Fargo was born when he was eighteen. Terror was his midwife, vengeance his first cry. Killing spawned Skye Fargo, ruthless, cold-blooded murder. Out of the acrid smoke of gunpowder still hanging in the air, he rose, cried out a promise never forgotten.

The Trailsman they began to call him all across the West: searcher, scout, hunter, the man who could see where others only looked, his skills for hire but not his soul, the man who lived each day to the fullest, yet trailed each tomorrow. Skye Fargo, the Trailsman, the seeker who could take the wildness of a land and the wanting of a woman and make them his own.

*West Texas, 1859—*
*A man's good name is his worth,*
*insured by a steady hand and hot lead.*

# 1

"Excuse me. Is this seat taken?"

The tall man in buckskins looked up from his study of the menu in the dining car of the *El Paso Flyer*.

The constant, back-and-forth swaying motion of the passenger train caused the woman who had asked the question to place a slim hand on the edge of his table to steady herself.

She was in her early twenties, attired for travel in pressed crinoline. Wisps of blond hair curled from beneath a stylish bonnet that matched her dress. Her eyes were blue and radiant with intelligence. Her prominent chin was slightly cleft, making her all the more attractive, in Fargo's opinion. She had a curvaceous figure, which the severity of her clothes could not conceal. Her breasts were upthrust, her hips round and firm. She held herself with a proud, almost aristocratic bearing, he noted, and yet she exuded a sunny, friendly-to-the-world openness.

A glance around told Fargo that the seat across the table from him was the only vacant one in the dining car.

The atmosphere in the dining car was comfortable and busy, abuzz with table chatter, the clink of silverware and dishes, and the comings and goings of efficient waiters. The Texas prairie, rolling by outside the train car windows, barren except for scrub brush and rock formations in the distance, was acquiring a golden patina as the sun descended lower in the western sky.

Fargo half-rose, gesturing. "Please, ma'am, have a seat. I'd appreciate the company."

Fargo had done all right financially by his last job and saw no reason not to return to El Paso in comfort. His horse, the beloved Ovaro stallion that was his one true friend, awaited him in El Paso, and he had enough folding money to take his time picking and choosing where his next dollars would come from. He was returning from having freelanced a job for the Rangers, who were undermanned in these parts. Fargo had signed on to escort a prisoner to Austin so the prisoner, a convicted murderer, could testify in an important trial. Fargo had earned his pay, which was another reason he didn't feel guilty about splurging on his return trip to El Paso. There had been the defendant's hired gunslingers, four of whom Fargo had had to kill, and several unsuccessful escape atempts that had to be dealt with, though fortunately not lethally. In the end, the prisoner had been delivered. Fargo had been paid.

And here he was, aboard a train due in El Paso at dawn, making the acquaintance of this charming young woman. He was glad he'd freshened up in his Pullman compartment before coming to dinner.

She was sizing him up exactly as he had her, assessing him and appearing satisfied with what she saw.

"Thank you. You're very kind." She seated herself primly across from him, as he settled back down. She extended a hand. "Lara Newton, of Boston, Massachusetts."

Her handshake conveyed confidence tempered with femininity, which he found arousing. A tingling sensation passed from her palm to his and went through him, warming his loins. He tried to keep this from showing in his expression.

"Skye Fargo, from down the road a piece."

"Down the road a piece?" She arched an eyebrow good-naturedly. "That's rather vague, isn't it?"

"With all due respect, ma'am, out here it isn't polite to ask questions about a person's background."

"I see." She regarded him with mild amusement. "Well then, the hell with being polite."

Fargo blinked. "Beg pardon, ma'am?"

"I said, the hell with being polite. I happen to be used to living my life flying in the face of social norms, Mr. Fargo. That's the way things were—I should say, are—with the family in Boston. And if I breach social etiquette in this quaint backwater of our great nation"—she nodded to the prairie speeding by outside the window—"then so be it. Frankly, I don't give a damn."

Fargo grinned. It made him look like a friendly bear. He had always liked spirited wenches.

"You're a plain spoken one, miss. Well, let's see now. This train's heading west, and my horse is waiting for me in El Paso. So you go ahead and decide where I'm from, if you've a mind to. But you might want to cut down on being so dang forward."

"I shouldn't act as I wish, you mean."

"I'm just saying."

"I'm a woman on a mission," she said, "and I've got money back home that can buy me out of any situation I get into, no matter the trouble."

"There's one kind of trouble it won't be able to buy you out of."

"And what's that?"

"Catching a bullet between those pretty eyes of yours," said Fargo. "That would be hard to buy your way out of, wouldn't it? On its way out it would make the back of your head look like strawberry jelly."

She winced. "Are you threatening me?"

"Threatening you? Heck, ma'am, I barely know you, and I'm starting to sort of hope it stays that way."

"Well."

He sighed. The tingling sensation within him had subsided, but not his appreciation of her beauty.

"Ma'am, I reckon if we're going to be traveling companions for the course of this meal, we may have to work at understanding what each other is saying."

She nodded in agreement. "I reckon," she said dryly.

A waiter appeared with a menu for her. She glanced it over as Fargo gave the waiter his order for a steak-and-potatoes dinner.

The woman across from him surprised Fargo when she handed the waiter the menu and said, "I'll have the same."

The waiter paused. "Begging your pardon, ma'am, but that's a mighty lot of food for a female, if you don't mind my saying so. Might I recommend the filet mignon?"

"I'm hungry," she said. Her eyes were locked on Fargo's when she added, "I have a big appetite." Lara Newton smiled a pretty, engaging smile. "I really should apologize, Mr. Fargo. I must seem awfully uppity to you."

"You've got your share of salt," Fargo conceded.

"May we begin again? It's been a long journey for

4

me. I'm afraid my nerves are frayed. I didn't mean to be cross. Will you forgive me?"

"No harm done," he said.

"The fact of the matter is, although I sometimes choose to behave like a shrew, I have grasped the rudiments of Western etiquette since about, oh, I suppose, Kansas City." Her expression grew serious. "I really wasn't trying to be impolite. The fact of the matter is, I'm looking for a man."

"You're looking for a man to do what?" he asked hopefully.

"I'm looking for a man to help me find my brother."

He hoped his disappointment was not visibly apparent.

"I need to know something about a man I hire. That's reasonable, isn't it?"

"Preferable, I'd say, from your perspective. And you want to hire me?"

"I believe I do, yes. I can offer you a substantial retainer."

"Yeah. You said Boston."

"My family is quite wealthy, as a matter of fact. They're aware of what I'm doing, I should say, although Father particularly disapproves of my undertaking."

"Finding your brother?"

"Yes. I've been on the lookout for the right man to help me since I first left Boston—a man who is resourceful, tough, hardened by experience and this environment." She nodded again to the darkening prairie beyond their dining car window. "A true man of the West," she concluded.

"I can't be the first able-bodied fellow you've encountered."

5

"Most of the men in the East, even the tough ones, wouldn't last a week out here," she said. "Some of the men I've considered along the way showed grit, but too often displayed a slowness of mind or a brutish side when I engaged them in conversation."

"The way you did with me?"

She nodded. "As I did with you."

"I reckon I'm flattered, although I've got to say that I believe you're moving this conversation along a mite fast."

"'Nimble' is the word you're looking for," she said. "That's what they called me at the boarding school Mother and Father sent me to. I was said to be a nimble conversationalist."

"Well, I'd say they pegged you about right," said Fargo. "So we're due in El Paso tomorrow morning and you still haven't found yourself the fellow you're looking for. And you're fixing to settle on me."

She leaned forward, reaching across the table to place a hand atop one of his. "I wouldn't put it that way. I'd have offered you a retainer had I seen you within five minutes of leaving Boston. You have an, oh, I don't know, an aura of rough-hewn ability not often seen in men back east, Mr. Fargo, or in many I've seen out here. You are the man I've been looking for."

That tingling sensation had returned, strange yet pleasant, when her palm touched the back of his rough hand there on the table. But it wasn't enough to keep him from thinking clearly.

"Ma'am, you ladies always surprise me, but you're a pip. Our meeting isn't coincidental, is it?"

Her high cheekbones rouged naturally. She indicated a windowed entrance at one end of the dining car, behind him. "I'm afraid I did peer in and observe

6

until every other seat was taken except this one." She smiled the merest hint of a smile. "Uh, if you don't mind my saying so, Mr. Fargo, no one seemed desirous of sitting with you."

Fargo glanced around them at the gentrified passengers enjoying their sumptuous repasts and jabbering among themselves while he sat clad in the buckskins of a trailsman, his Colt holstered at his right hip.

"Imagine that. Reckon I'm not what these people are looking for."

"Well, I'm not them. You make a strong first impression, Mr. Fargo. My first impression of you is precisely that of the man I have been seeking. And may I add that when it comes to first impressions, mine always prove accurate. Always."

He held up both hands in a friendly, placating gesture. "Miss, far be it from me to question anything you say about yourself."

The *Flyer* was noted for its outstanding cuisine, and when dinner arrived, Fargo's steak was proof enough for him, seasoned and grilled to perfection. There was a natural pause in their conversation as amenities were exchanged over the tastiness of their dinner.

Fargo observed the "lady" attacking her steak as if she hadn't eaten in days, with an intensity of purpose that temporarily precluded conversation. He couldn't help but chuckle again, this time inwardly. He wasn't sure yet if it would be advantageous for him to let Miss Newton of Boston know how much she tickled his fancy. He found her peculiar brand of forthright intelligence and sass extremely appealing, and she was real easy on the eyes. And it counted that it was family business that had brought her to this hostile environment more than a thousand miles from her home. Fargo had always placed a high value on allegiance to family, which Lara's behavior embodied.

After several minutes of eating, he said, between chews, "Tell me about your brother."

# 2

Lara was close to finishing off her steak. She didn't pause in her chewing. "Do you know Fort Survival?"

"I do," said Fargo. "That's an Army outpost established to keep a lid on things up northeast of El Paso. Lot of trouble around those parts."

She paused, a forkful of steak halfway to her mouth. "You know the region?"

"I've been through there. Fort Survival is under Colonel Talbot's command."

She lowered the fork. Her gaze sharpened. "You know the colonel?"

"I scouted for him up in Colorado a few years back when the Utes were on the warpath. Colonel Talbot, he's all right."

"You've served with him?"

"No, ma'am. A scout is his own man. That's the only way I ever do anything. Contract work for the government is what they call scouting in their fancy paperwork. But yeah, the colonel and me, we've taken enemy fire together. Like I say, he's a good man. Now what does the colonel have to do with your brother?"

She set her fork down and pushed away the nearly finished dinner as if having abruptly lost interest in the meal she'd been devouring.

"Jeff is a lieutenant stationed at Fort Survival. They say he deserted."

"They?"

"Well, the Army sent the letter to my parents. But it was Colonel Talbot who filed the initial report. They contacted my family because they thought Jeff might return home. Deserters often do, I'm told."

"You don't think he deserted."

"I *know* he didn't." She removed her hand from his and placed it, palm down, above her left breast, in the region of her heart. "I *feel* it. That's how I know. I know my brother, Mr. Fargo. He's a good soldier. Fort Survival is his first duty assignment. I attended his graduation at West Point this spring. He's my older brother. I've always looked up to him. Jeff has never given any endeavor less than his all."

"But that wasn't enough to convince the Army that he didn't desert."

"I'm not trying to convince the Army," she said, with a lift of her cleft chin. "I am merely stating for you what I know to be fact. My brother, Lieutenant Jeffrey Newton, did not desert as is alleged."

"What's your theory?"

Her forehead furrowed. "I don't know. That's why I've traveled all of this distance. That's why I'm offering to pay you. I need the abilities of someone like you, Mr. Fargo."

"Your family believes the Army?"

Her eyes lowered. "They do. Jeff disappeared from Fort Survival without a trace. You see, they have reason to suspect the worst. Our mother does want to believe in him, but Father . . . well, it's true that Jeffrey was wild and irresponsible as a boy. But he's a man now. He has mastered self-discipline. He is no deserter."

"What does the Army say happened?"

"That's the most aggravating part. You can't imagine what a Herculean effort it took for me to even learn the name of Jeff's commander and where he was stationed. I had to go all the way to Washington, and if you think I was impolite earlier, well then, you may believe me when I say that the gentlemen in Washington were happy to see me go after tangling with me."

Fargo chuckled. "I'm not sure I want to know what you're like when you're on a tear. I expect they would have preferred to have tangled with a mama lion."

"It's my family's right to know what happened to Jeffrey. In any event, I returned to Boston with at least the information I sought, or rather as much as the Army was willing to divulge. A lot of good it did me. Father refuses to budge in his acceptance of the notion that Jeffrey is a deserter. To quote my father, 'the Army and the Newton name are well rid of him.'"

Fargo stroked his chin. "That does sound harsh, coming from blood kin."

"Father is a harsh man." She lifted her eyes to his and feminine determination stared at him. "There's a young man waiting for me in Boston who thinks we are to be married. And of course Father is apoplectic over my behavior. Mother understands. I felt as if I was seeing my parents for the last time when I left Boston. I don't know if I shall ever go back. There's something about . . . out here. The people behave differently, in a way I fancy, and wish to learn more about. I think you Westerners are different from us Easterners because of this big land."

Beyond their window a purple mantle was claiming the land, softening the distant rock formations into inky smudges. Stars twinkled in a darkening sky.

"Big and dangerous," said Fargo. "There's real trouble where you're going. There are ranchers, homesteaders, miners, and miles and miles of wilderness. And it's not just the Indians causing the grief. There are bands of white outlaws, too, and Mexican *banditos*, long riders up from across the Rio Grande. Word I've heard along the trail is that the patrols out of Fort Survival are keeping the peace up there, but just barely. It's a real dicey situation you're heading into, miss."

"Please call me Lara."

"Lara."

This time her smile was of the Mona Lisa variety. "I like the way my name sounds when you say it."

He didn't know what to say to that, so he said, "Does anyone know that you're traveling out here like this?"

She nodded. "Mr. G. Chadwell Sanford. I telegraphed him from Kansas City and informed him of my arrival."

"Quite a moniker," Fargo couldn't help but note. "G. Chadwell Sanford." He rolled the name around in his mouth as if he tasted it. "No Junior or the Third to top it off?"

She chuckled pleasantly. "Mr. Sanford is a transplanted Easterner. I suppose our ways seem a bit stuffy out here." Her smile quirked self-consciously. "I should perhaps interject at this point that my family is, uh, quite wealthy."

Fargo smiled. "So I didn't think you were from the wrong side of the tracks."

"I mean wealthy as in, the Newtons are one of the richest families in the nation," she said. "Mr. Sanford is one of my father's business associates, a solicitor, an old family friend for whom I have a great deal of affection. I've known Mr. Sanford since I was a child. He's been . . . 'avuncular,' I think the word is."

"Whatever you say, Lara."

Fargo could not bring himself to admit to her that he did not know the meaning of the word "avuncular." He would have to look that one up.

"If he's an associate of your father's," asked Fargo, "why did you tell him you're coming to El Paso?"

"Mr. Sanford is important in his own right, and wields a considerable amount of influence in this region. You will accompany me to Fort Survival, and Mr. Sanford will hopefully provide us with information and suggestions."

From the corner of his eye, Fargo suddenly detected vague movement outside the train window, a shifting in the gathering darkness that shouldn't have been there.

It was dark enough by now so that the windows reflected the dining car's well-lighted interior. But something stirred in his subconscious. He was certain that he'd caught the suggestion of something beyond the glass, out there in the night.

Lara misinterpreted his hesitation in responding.

"That is," she said, "I assume you are willing to take the job I'm offering you. I will pay you well. I really do need an assistant, Mr. Fargo."

He watched the darkness beyond the window, squinting, but could see nothing.

"Wrong word," he finally said. "You're hiring yourself a scout. And a bodyguard, looks like."

She started to turn in her seat to peer out the window in the same direction she saw him peering.

"Thank you, Mr. Fargo. But what—"

He saw clearly then, through the window, what had been only the suggestion of movement before.

A horseman was riding hell-for-leather, alongside the train. He rode low in the saddle and wildly whipped the horse with a quirt, side to side, urging the mount onward toward the front of the train.

Fargo had only a second to glimpse the man as the rider drew abreast of the train, close enough for light from inside the row of dining car windows to spill out across him. Then the horse bolted forward and the horseman disappeared from sight.

The train began slowing with a jarring lurch, rocking everyone in their seats. Startled shouts and gasps of surprise filled the dining car.

Fargo realized instantly what was happening. The train engine was being commandeered. Horsemen had swooped down on the train from both sides under cover of darkness. The train was slowing only heartbeats after he'd spotted the horseman. There had not been enough time for the man to reach the locomotive, much less to leap to it from his galloping horse and command the engineer to stop the train. This meant that there were already one or more men aboard the locomotive. The man Fargo had seen was riding backup, or was racing to catch up, lagging behind schedule. The realization fell into place even before Fargo had righted himself from the lurch caused by the train's sudden slowing. He'd done his share of tracking train robbers, and he knew their methods well.

Around him, the diners' initial surprise gave way to petulant mumbling as the train ground to a halt. A glass of water spilled here and there. There were terse calls of *"Waiter! Waiter!"* while others demanded to know the reason for this delay. The waiters could only shrug.

"What's happening?" asked Lara. "I don't understand."

Fargo stood, reaching for his holstered Colt.

"Trouble," he growled. "Stay down."

She did not heed his warning. Her expression flared with surprise when she saw something over his shoulder. She raised an arm, pointing frantically.

"Look out!"

Fargo whirled, tracking the Colt around with him.

He froze when he saw the man standing in the rear doorway of the dining car.

The stocky man wore a broad-brimmed hat and a black duster. A bandana concealed the lower half of his face. He held a sawed-off shotgun aimed at Fargo.

"Hold it right there, pilgrim, and drop the iron," the man ordered, "or I'll blow your innards across everyone sitting here. Only reason you ain't a dead man standing is that you can maybe tell me what I needs to know. Now drop it."

Fargo released the Colt. It clunked onto the carpeted floor.

The train had ground to a stop. From up ahead, the locomotive could be heard steaming and wheezing, a mechanical giant stalled on the prairie. A trace of coal smoke, usually carried off on the slipstream when the train was in motion, drifted into the dining car, nipping at nostrils. The atmosphere in the car crackled with tension.

The door at the front end swung open. Fargo heard spurs jangle as someone else stepped inside.

The new arrival called to the man in the rear doorway. "Didn't have to kill the engineer. How you making out?"

The masked man, aiming the shotgun at Fargo, said, "I've got it under control." He glared at Fargo along the length of the shotgun's double barrels. "Don't I, pilgrim?"

Fargo kept his hands out from his sides, clearly indicating that he was offering no resistance. "No one here wants to get hurt, least of all me," he said.

Mumbled assents from the surrounding tables. Fargo was the only passenger who had openly worn a weapon during dinner. Everyone else sat frozen in place, holding their collective breath.

"Well, I'm right happy to hear that," said the man wearing the mask. "If the person I'm looking for is here, why, I'll just take her with me, and me and my men will be on our way."

"Who are you looking for?" Fargo asked. He stood in the aisle next to his chair, shielding Lara from the first outlaw with his body while getting a look at the man who had boxed him in from the other side. This outlaw matched the first, including toting a sawed-off shotgun, except his duster was yellow. Fargo somehow knew what the first one's response would be before it was spoken.

"We're looking for Lara Newton. If she's here, turn her over." The man's shotgun, and his unblinking eyes, remained on Fargo from a distance of some ten feet away. "Who's that sitting behind you, mister?"

"Matter of fact," said Fargo, "it just happens to be the young lady you're looking for." He turned and gallantly extended a hand, offering to assist Lara to her feet. "Miss Newton," he said, "some gentlemen to see you."

Lara drew back against the window, cringing as if he were a repugnant reptile.

"You lousy, no good—" she started to say.

Positioned so neither outlaw could see what he was doing, Fargo bent down slightly, quickly, allowing his extended hand to drop and draw the Arkansas toothpick from inside his left boot. He twisted at the waist and flung the knife, overhand, at the nearest outlaw.

The knife sunk to the hilt in the man's heart. He emitted a strange little gurgling noise from behind his mask, then slumped to both knees. He held onto the shotgun, but it was no longer aimed at Fargo. The shotgun boomed, a deafening thunderclap within the con-

16

fines of the train car, blowing a hole into the aisle floor. Then the man pitched forward, dead.

Pandemonium erupted. Women screamed. Men cursed. Passengers leaped aside, overturning tables.

Fargo whirled back in the direction of the outlaw at the far end of the car, throwing himself to the floor, reaching for his Colt, clasping his hand around its grip, a finger around the trigger. But the outlaw was already drawing a bead on Fargo, and there would be no time to pull his pistol up. He was a dead man.

There was the crack of a gunshot.

Fargo flinched instinctually, prepared to be blown apart in a millisecond by a load of buckshot from the shotgun, before his mind grasped that it was hardly a shotgun blast. Rather, it was the report of a handgun!

A purple hole appeared in the outlaw's forehead. The walls to either side of the doorway behind him were painted with gore from the exit wound. The shotgun dropped from his fingers. He pitched to the floor.

Fargo rose, Colt in hand.

Lara sat with her back to the window. She sat erect, as if her backbone was of steel, and there was a steely glint in her eyes. There was a short-nosed revolver in her hand, which she had obviously drawn from the open purse on her lap. A wisp of smoke curled from the gun barrel.

"I'm a member of the women's league of the Boston Shooting Club," she said.

"And damn lucky for me," said Fargo. "Much obliged, ma'am. I owe you one."

"You were going to call me Lara. And thank you, Skye."

The hubbub surrounding them tapered off to mumbling of concern and confusion, but not panic.

"Lara, it's not over yet," said Fargo. He raised his

voice and spoke to those around them. "Folks, stay calm. Don't leave this car. Those boys we killed weren't alone. And here's Exhibit A."

A masked outlaw, this one armed with a Winchester, entered the far end of the dining car, looking for someone to shoot at.

Fargo killed the man with a single headshot.

Panic erupted again, but a mass exit toward the front of the car was aborted when two more masked outlaws poured in from the direction of where they had been searching the rest of the train. They stormed in, their pistols blazing in Fargo's direction.

Fargo heard a bullet zip by within a fraction of an inch of his left ear. He took aim on the first man through and sent a bullet into the man's chest. The man's body tumbled onto a table, which collapsed under his weight. Simultaneously, Fargo and the second man fired at each other. For the moment, the last sound Fargo heard was the ringing of another gunshot from Lara's pistol as she let loose a shot of her own. Then, suddenly, he felt as if he'd been kicked in the head by a mule.

His senses reeled and for a moment he thought he was going to die as he fell, but the impact of his head striking the carpet cleared his senses. His head throbbed with pain, and blood was seeping from a wound at the side of his head.

He forced himself to not move, to play possum. This was extremely difficult, considering that the trickle of blood seeping into his eye was stinging like hell. He fought down a nearly overwhelming urge to brush the blood away, and squinted through his good eye.

The man stalked straight toward Lara. She aimed her pistol at him and squeezed the trigger, but there was only a *click!* Her gun had jammed. The man laughed.

He made a swatting motion, and the pistol flew from her hand.

The outlaw grasped her by an arm. "Looks like I'm the last of our boys left." He yanked Lara to her feet. "Reckon that means I collect a full share for taking care of you."

As she was being dragged from where she'd been sitting, Lara sent a horrified glance down at Fargo.

"My God. Oh my God! It's my fault. You've killed him! Oh, I'm so sorry, Mr. Fargo!"

The outlaw dragged her past the onlookers, toward the door.

"Shut the hell up or I'll bat you around some, and don't think I won't. You're coming with me."

When they reached the door, Fargo willed himself to his feet, brushing away the blood from his eye. His vision was blurred, his surroundings were unsteady, but he clearly discerned the outlaw, with Lara in tow, about to exit the dining car.

"Hold it," Fargo said. "You're not taking her anywhere. Let her go."

The outlaw flung Lara aside, bringing his pistol around at Fargo. "So I've got to kill you again, pilgrim?"

"Not today," said Fargo.

In a flash, Fargo drew, aimed, and blew the bastard's head off.

He was vaguely aware of the man dropping, and of Lara hurrying toward him, concern on her lovely face. The world became a silent place and began fading to gray.

"You called me Mr. Fargo," he heard himself say. "I thought it was going to be Skye and Lara."

He lost consciousness before hearing her reply.

# 3

The jolt of pain that awoke him was real enough to tell Fargo that he was no longer dreaming.

He was alive and in a world of pain. A throbbing agony in his temples only worsened when he opened his eyes. He was staring at a white ceiling, so he figured he must be indoors. Figuring that much out was a start, but he had to stop the pain before he could know or do anything else.

Remaining in a prone position, he willed his arms to draw up, sending the pain from his head scalding across his upper body. He pressed his fingertips with as much pressure as he could muster, drumming the fingertips in small circles at key pressure points. Sluggishly at first, then in a rush, the agony in his skull subsided to a more tolerable level. He worked the pressure points some more and the fire in his veins cooled. His senses awakened.

He was lying in bed with the covers pulled up to his chin. And he was butt naked under the covers!

Fargo ceased massaging the pressure points. He gingerly felt the gauze bandage wrapped around his head. The bedroom smelled of disinfectant. He tilted his head sideways on a feather pillow. He saw a window flanked by ornate oak dressers, and a slate-gray sky beyond. Trees were bending in a stiff wind. Pain surged through him from having turned his head. He waited for the pain to subside, then brought his head to look up, on his way to survey what was on the other side of the bed.

He paused in looking up. A face hovered over his, someone leaning forward, looking down, and for a second he wondered if maybe he was dreaming again. Blonde curls surrounded the woman's face. Big blue eyes regarded him with concern. He blinked, which hurt. But the pain told him that this was no dream.

With her Mona Lisa smile, Lara Newton said, "Well, hello there." Then she spoke to someone else. "Mr. Sanford, he's regaining consciousness."

Fargo became aware of blurry movement behind Lara. He started to sit up. The jolt of pain was like a body blow, and he sunk back onto the pillow with a frustrated grunt before trying again. The jolting pain served to sharpen his senses, and he became fully awake.

He said to the face above, "Hello, Lara." His voice sounded weak. He cleared his throat. "Reckon you know what I'm wondering about." This time he was starting to sound like himself again.

"You mean," said tartly, "where the hell you are?"

A male cough sounded from the blurry figure. "Lara, please. That's no way for a lady to talk."

Lara drew back from Fargo.

"I killed a man on that train last night, Mr. Sanford. I may no longer be entitled the distinction of being a lady."

A phlegmy voice harrumphed. "My dear child, I'm not quite certain what to make of any of this, showing up on my doorstep with this wounded man."

"But I telegraphed you that I was coming, and you

wired back that I could avail myself of your hospitality."

"But of course. That hasn't changed. You're most welcome here, my dear, you know that. But this man you brought with you, this ruffian—"

"This ruffian saved my life."

Fargo decided to forego trying to sit up for the time being. He had regained enough of a clear head to say, "Howdy there, Mr. Sanford. Mind stepping up so I can get a look at who I'm talking to?"

A portly gent in his late fifties stepped to the foot of the bed. He had muttonchop sideburns, fluffy-white like fleecy clouds, and a halo of thin white hair around a bald spot resembling feathers encircling an egg. Sanford was rosy cheeked, but his eyes and the set of his jaw were pugnacious, like a streetfighter.

"How do you do, Mr. Fargo?" The tone was civil, not cordial. "You are in a guest bedroom in my home in El Paso. You were brought here by my niece—that's what I call Lara—after the train arrived. I'm sorry if I sound ungrateful. I'm not. I will say that I've been reliably informed that you performed valiantly and gallantly in Miss Newton's defense. I most assuredly thank you for saving her life."

"I was saving my own in the process," said Fargo, "and thanks for the hospitality. I'll be on my way soon enough. And you're right. I am a ruffian."

Another harrumph from Sanford.

"My apologies, sir. It's just that, well, I, uh, happen to be a prominent businessman in this community, and, uh, the quality of the people who stay in my home is . . . well, I'm certain you understand."

"Hey, I get it all the time," said Fargo. "No riffraff. You've got to keep up a front."

Lara stepped forward. She clutched the same purse, Fargo noted, that last night had held her pistol.

"But this isn't right! Please reconsider, sir."

Sanford smiled. "My dear, in the interests of your family name and your father's investments out here, it is you who must reconsider. You must forgive my candor. Mr. Fargo and I have taken different paths in life and have reached different destinations, but we are men of the world who understand each other." He glanced in Fargo's direction. "Am I not right, sir? Please tell Lara that I am not the ogre I seem to be. Women do not have a head for this sort of cold-blooded business."

"I've thanked you for your hospitality," said Fargo. "Reckon I don't know you well enough to say much else."

Sanford's eyes narrowed. "Honesty repays honesty. Quite right, sir. Quite right." He turned to Lara. "My dear, would you mind allowing Mr. Fargo and I a few minutes of private conversation?"

Lara flinched, as if wholly unprepared for the request. But years of upper-crust upbringing paid off, Fargo noted. She betrayed no emotion. She retained a feminine dignity and humility that Fargo saw through only because he had seen her kill a man last night.

She gave the slightest curtsy without a glance at Fargo. "Whatever you wish, sir. Excuse me, gentlemen. I'll be in the library."

"Hold on," said Fargo. He made another effort to sit up. This time he succeeded. The pain that wracked his body this time was a momentary thing. When he was sitting upright, his back against the headboard, he said, "Mr. Sanford, it'd be my privilege to have a private confab with a fella as important as you. But I would like a word alone with Miss Newton first."

A slight flinch, as if he'd been physically slapped, indicated that Sanford was unprepared for this turn in the conversation.

"Well, I suppose," he sighed unenthusiastically, before withdrawing from the bedroom.

Lara sat upon the bed, beside Fargo, close enough for the curve of her thigh to press against his, separated only by the bedcovers and the fabric of her dress. Beneath the covers, Fargo felt his naked manhood stir.

Lara brushed aside a lank of his hair from his forehead, mussed while he slept.

"You were a brave warrior last night. You were like a knight in the books I read as a schoolgirl."

Fargo growled. "Yeah, they were ruffians too. Pardon me for saying so, hon, and I don't much give a damn if I am under his roof, but I don't cotton to that old bird, and if I was you, I'd watch my back."

Her fingertips lingered near his gauze-covered wound. "I wish you could know and respect each other for who each of you truly is."

"Do you know who he truly is?"

"I told you, I've known him since I was a child."

"When's the last time you saw him before last night?"

"Why, I haven't actually seen Mr. Sanford in, oh, I guess it's been seven years now. But he calls me his niece because he and my father are like brothers."

"Has your father seen Sanford since he came west?"

Her expression clouded. "I'm not sure I know what you mean."

"People change. Why are your father and this man like brothers?"

"They were mining partners when they were

young. That's where the money first came from. It was my father's claim, but Mr. Sanford was Father's best friend in the camp and they worked the claim together, as I remember the story. They stood off a gang of claim jumpers in a bloody battle that lasted for several days, the two of them holding off more than a dozen of them. They were both wounded, but they held onto the mine."

"Something like that would make men into brothers," Fargo conceded. "What does Sanford know about last night?"

She frowned. "Only that you're a man to be reckoned with in the way you dispatched those desperados."

"Nicely put. Does he know that you hired me to help you find out what happened to your brother?"

Her frown lines deepened. "No. For some reason I didn't mention that to him. He knows the rest of what happened. But no one knows about our conversation in the dining car before things started happening."

"Let's keep it that way," said Fargo. "Okay, I'm ready. Show the old boy in."

"Skye, please don't be unkind to him. Mr. Sanford's only concern is my welfare."

"If that's the case, he's got nothing to worry about from me." He patted her sweet thigh. "I'll do my best, but don't forget that I am a ruffian."

She sighed. "I'm beginning to see the side of you that is incorrigible."

"You and your big words."

She emitted an unladylike grunt of frustration, then rose from the bed and left the room, leaving the door open.

Sanford entered the room. Closing the door behind

him, he began pacing back and forth at the foot of Fargo's bed.

"Now then, Fargo, I do trust that you know that I am obliged to you for your actions last night on my niece's behalf."

"We've been over that," said Fargo. "Why are we talking alone?"

"I merely wish to make you aware of the fact that you have gotten yourself involved with a young woman about whom powerful people feel most protective."

"I sort of got that idea."

Sanford continued his pacing. "The fact of the matter is, Lara's father had detectives trailing her from the time she first boarded the train to leave Boston."

"Is that right?" said Fargo. "So where the hell were they last night? That young woman you call your niece is the only one who gave me any backup."

"Unfortunately, Lara somehow managed to elude the detectives during a train change in Cincinnati."

Fargo felt a tight grin tug at the corners of his mouth. "That's not too far along the line, is it?"

"I understand you were dining with Lara when last's night's troubles began."

"I was, but it was a chance meeting. The seat across from me was the only one vacant when she came in."

"And has she told you why she is traveling west?"

"We didn't get that far. But now that you mention it, I reckon I am kind of curious. She's a long way from home."

Sanford paused in his pacing. He glared at Fargo. There was nothing cherubic about him now. He looked like an old shark.

"The point is, sir, that none of this is your concern. I am not denying Lara's considerable resourcefulness, but the fact of the matter is that she is now back under the protection of her family, whether she likes it or not. She will be amply protected from here on, without your assistance."

"Like in Cincinnati?"

Sanford reached into an inside breast pocket of his coat, and for a moment Fargo thought the man was about to draw a pistol and shoot him without further explanation. Fargo realized this and also realized that despite his aches and pains, he was back on an even keel should he need to act. He felt his muscles bunching under the bedcovers, and he was ready to leap at Sanford. Relief washed over him when the man produced not a weapon, but a stack of what looked to be freshly minted currency.

Sanford placed the stack of paper money on a bedside table, within Fargo's reach.

"There's one thousand dollars," said Sanford. "It's yours, trail bum. You got lucky. Call it a token of the Newton family's appreciation for your good deed."

"You mean," said Fargo, regarding the money, but leaving it untouched, "it's a payoff to get out of town."

Sanford smiled briefly. "If you wish. Very well, let us continue to be candid."

"Yeah, let us."

"I want you on the next train out of El Paso." Sanford indicated the money. "That is how much it's worth to me, and to the girl's family."

Fargo continued to regard the stack of currency. "A substantial amount."

Sanford produced and glanced at a gold-plated watch. "I'm due to preside over an important business engagement on the other side of town, and I'm already behind schedule. I trust you will excuse the brevity of this exchange."

"Trust away," said Fargo. "Hell, I prefer it that way."

Sanford glared at Fargo a moment longer, without speaking, then wheeled about and left the bedroom. Fargo heard the man's boots clumping down a flight of stairs.

Fargo brought his legs around to the floor and got to his feet. Stabbing aches and pains here and there, but manageable. When he was standing, he tilted and leaned against the nearest wall with an outstretched arm. He drew in deep breaths. When the room steadied, he stood upright and found his equilibrium returned.

He heard a heavy door open and close downstairs, and then he heard a buggy riding away from the house. Now that he was on his feet, he saw his buckskins, looking freshly washed, and his boots, freshly polished, by a chair, with his hat, on the other side of a dresser.

He grabbed hold of the britches, stepped into them, and was in the process of drawing them up when the bedroom opened and he heard a woman's sharp intake of breath.

"Oh, good gracious! Excuse me, Mr. Fargo!"

Fargo made sure the britches were secure, then turned to face Lara Newton, who stood in the bedroom doorway with one hand on the door handle, and shock widening her eyes.

Fargo reached for his shirt. "Sorry, ma'am . . . uh, I mean, Lara. Didn't mean for you to see my bare backside like that."

She stepped into the bedroom, closing the door.

She stood with her back against the wood panel. She was blushing.

"I'm sorry. I should have knocked. But wait. What are you doing?" She rushed across to extend an arm that stayed him from raising the shirt over his head. "Mr. Fargo, you've been seriously injured! You're not ready to—"

Fargo stood there, bare-chested, barefoot, clad only in his buckskin britches. He nodded at the stack of money on the bedside table.

"Your so-called uncle just offered me a big payoff to skedaddle out of town on the first thing smoking."

"But, Skye . . . you're working for me!"

He chuckled, touching her lightly on both arms. He planted a chaste kiss on her forehead. "Relax, kitten. You told me that unc doesn't know about that."

"He doesn't."

"Well," said Fargo, "that's why he made the offer. I didn't say I was going to accept it. And while we're on the subject of offers, you and I were interrupted before we finished discussing your offer to me last night. Since I'm working for you, reckon I'm curious as to how much I'm being paid."

Her blush receded, but she was obviously trying to keep her eyes averted, not altogether successfully, from the heavily muscled, naked male chest before her.

"May I ask how much is in that stack of bills?"

"One thousand dollars, if your uncle is to be believed."

"Why don't you like Mr. Sanford?"

"We'll talk about that later. You're not trying to dodge the question of my retainer, are you?" Fargo chuckled. "Wouldn't surprise me if you were. You do seem to have grown up around sharpies."

Her chin lifted. "I don't think I like your attitude."

"My attitude's not for sale. You hired me to help you find out what happened to your brother. The question is, how much?"

"Very well," said Lara. "I will pay you two thousand dollars. I can have the money wired to any bank in the United States." Her arm remained upon the buckskin shirt he held, blocking him from donning it. "But what are you doing, Skye?"

"You and I have got places to go and things to do," said Fargo. "Sanford just told me that he's on his way to the other side of town for some business. I want us to use that time."

She touched his gauze head wrapping with gentle fingers.

"But what about this? I don't see how you can be strong enough so soon. Really, Skye, I must insist that you not undertake such a dangerous job until you truly are strong enough to function."

The nearness of her filled Fargo with even more energy. He flung the shirt aside.

Fargo scooped her off her feet, taking her completely by surprise. He hadn't missed how her eyes couldn't resist his bare chest, and he'd sensed a mutual attraction from the moment they'd met on the train.

She gave a quiet little squeal of surprise and delight. She held on to him, hugging his shoulders. A few paces to the bed and he lowered her onto it, following her down across the thrown-back covers, pinning her beneath him.

They were both laughing. Then their lips met in a steamy kiss. When the kiss broke, they gulped in air like two people who had been submerged under water for too long.

He looked down into her excited, dancing eyes.

"Strong enough?" he asked.

Her arms remained around him, clasping his back. Their lips locked again.

Her tongue darted sensuously, caressing his tongue. "Oh, yes, Skye, *yes!* You *have* made your point!" She was panting as if from having run a long distance. "My goodness, you're a big and strong man. You're right, damn you. I couldn't take my eyes off you. I want you. I *need* you!"

He kissed her throat and enjoyed feeling her body quake.

"I didn't know they raised gals so friendly up in Boston."

"It's a cold climate," she said. "A girl has to learn a few tricks to keep warm."

Fargo paused then, with her in his arms. Every curve of her body was pressed against his, there upon the bed. He felt the ripeness of her body beneath the fabric of her clothes. Heat emanated from her.

Fargo paused to say, "Lara Newton, you are really something."

She tightened her hold on him, whispering breathily in his ear. "Skye Fargo, I *want* something and, mister, it's *you!*"

"Let's see what we can manage," said Fargo.

He was not about to actually take this filly all the way, right here under her "uncle's" roof, much as he would have liked to. If a man gets to serious lovemaking, and Fargo knew no other kind, he tends to get lax paying attention to other things. This was strange turf to Fargo. There would be servants about, and who knew if Sanford was even telling the truth about leaving for a while? It would be a complication Fargo didn't need to get caught making love to the wealthy heiress from Boston under these circumstances.

On the other hand, half-measures could be satisfying if not fulfilling. Additionally, Fargo never liked to pass an opportunity for intimacy with a beautiful woman.

Stretching her across the bedcovers, holding her securely with an arm around her waist, he eased his other hand up to the front of her dress and cupped her left breast, palming it with firm gentleness, shifting his weight, positioning one of his knees against the V of her legs.

"Oh, goodness!" she mewed.

"Y'know, I really do feel fine," said Fargo.

He felt the heat of her crotch against his knee through the fabric of her dress and petticoat. He leaned forward and applied the best kind of pressure there was.

She clamped her legs around the knee and began gyrating against it, making tiny, rapid whimpering sounds. She shifted her body back and forth, her thigh against the front of his britches, rubbing his maleness, which had grown hard and throbbing, palpable through the buckskin. She rocked her body this way and that beneath him. They were both breathing hard. Rubbing like this for only seconds made her body quiver and tremble. Her hips bucked uncontrollably with spasms of pleasure.

She moaned. "Oh, Skye!"

Her climax, and the way she rubbed her thigh against his hardness, made him groan. He felt himself approaching his own climax.

She rubbed her thigh harder and faster against the bulge in his buckskins. "Come on, baby," she coaxed in a fierce, breathy whisper. "All for me, baby. Let me feel it shoot. Do it, Skye!"

He gripped her hips with both hands and stopped her body from rocking. He bit his lip to hold in his moan. But he managed to stop himself just short of the point of no return.

"Cool down, sugar," he whispered, restraining her provocative movement. "One will have to do you for now, but it's nice to know you're a little minx."

She grinned up at him impishly. "I am for you, big fella. But what about you?" She reached down and felt the front of his britches. "You're already losing it!"

"That's the way I want it, kitten."

"But—"

He lifted himself from her and got back to his feet. His erection had disappeared. "That one was on me because you're a hot piece."

She sat and stared at him as if he were from another planet. "You, Skye Fargo, are the damnedest man."

"When I go that far with you, it's going to be the way God planned it," said Fargo.

A pleasurable tremor shuddered through her visibly as she sat there on the bed, watching him put on his clothes. She eyed him with a gaze somewhere between amazement and suspicion. Then she took a deep breath and attempted to fix her hair.

"Thank you, Skye. That was incredible."

He extended a hand and drew her close to him, his arms wrapped around her.

"You'll get more of it if it's what you want, and so will I," he promised. He delivered an affectionate slap to her rump for emphasis, followed by a deep, wet kiss. "But right now, Lara, we've got other things to talk about."

33

# 4

"What other things do we have to talk about?" asked Lara.

Beyond the bedroom window the monolithic shadow of the big house could be seen lengthening across the well-manicured grounds.

Fargo continued donning his buckskin shirt, tucking its tails in. Funny, he thought. Even though he was not watching her directly, he could see from the corner of his eye that, the more he covered up, the more closely Lara was observing his every move, as if now it was permissible to drink in a sight that obviously pleased her.

He sat on a straight-backed chair and reached for his boot. Fact of the matter was, he'd now have gone on with Lara, looking for her brother, without being paid. But though he may not have been G. Chadwell Sanford, Fargo was businessman enough not to tell her that. She had a sharpie streak herself that nicely complemented her other capabilities, but not at the expense of her femininity. Aches and pains rippled across his muscles, all over his body, like rushing cockroaches—a critical irritation, real unpleasant. But with every movement, his pain was receding. With one boot pulled on, he reached for the other.

He said, "I had a pistol last night. I remember using it."

She stood abruptly. "I'm sorry. Mr. Sanford asked for it to be kept out of sight. He said it was unpleasant to display a weapon openly in a home."

"Reasonable," said Fargo, slipping on the other boot.

She went to a bureau and opened one of the drawers.

Fargo retrieved his hat, placing it on his head cocked at the proper angle. There was still the dull, throbbing ache of the wound, but beyond that he felt pretty much back to normal, especially when Lara returned to him and handed him his holstered pistol wrapped in the cartridge belt. He buckled the gunbelt around his waist.

He made a quick inspection of the Colt, snapping the cylinder open with a flick of his wrist. The gun was fully loaded. He checked the firing pin. Then he checked his reflexes, twirling the pistol at blinding speed. He performed and repeated the border shift, flipping the pistol from hand to hand. Satisfied, he holstered the gun at his hip.

"Here's what I want to talk about." He pitched his voice to a near whisper. "I intend to investigate Sanford, as part of my job of working for you, of course. Something about this deal stinks to high heaven."

She nodded glumly. "I'm thinking I know what you mean. Those outlaws last night were looking for me specifically. Only one person was supposed to know that I was on that train . . . my uncle."

"He's not your uncle," said Fargo. "And he could well be the man who wants you dead or at least kept under wraps. Sure, he fought with your father a long time ago. But that last boy I sent to glory on the train last night talked about collecting for taking care of you. Those weren't run-of-the-mill train robbers. They were coming for you, and they were on someone's payroll."

"And you think that someone is Uncle . . . is Mr. Sanford."

"Don't play it cute," said Fargo. "I can tell from your voice that you think the same thing."

"But why would he want harm to befall me? It can only have something to do with my reason for being here, my search to find out what happened to my brother."

"That's the obvious connection." Fargo crossed the bedroom and stood by the door, moving on the balls of his feet, making no noise. "Or maybe Sanford's been up to no good, swindling your father out of profits from their Western enterprises. He doesn't want you to find out about it. Or maybe there's more than one reason he wants you muzzled." Fargo turned the door handle. Before opening the door, he turned to Lara with a grin. "On the other hand, maybe muzzling a chili pepper like you isn't such a bum notion. You tend to stir things up when a feller least expects it."

She regarded him with amusement from across the room. "Name a woman who doesn't. And I must say, you're being rather impertinent."

"I thought we discussed attitude," said Fargo.

"And as I recall," said Lara, "it was you who picked me up like the caveman you are and tossed me onto that bed. It takes two to muss the covers, Fargo."

"Shush," he said. He cracked open the door less than a quarter inch, just enough to spy in either direction of the second floor hallway. Polished oak floors were covered with Mexican rugs. Closed doors lined one wall, which faced a wide stairway to the foyer downstairs. Fargo closed the door and looked back at

Lara. "How many servants and employees are we going to have to deal with?"

"Deal with?"

"I need a distraction," said Fargo. "How many people are we talking bout?"

She crossed to stand with him at the door. "What time is it?"

He brought out his watch, glanced at its face and snapped it shut, pocketing it. "Just past five."

"That means the house servants have been gone for almost an hour. There's Jake, the handyman, who lives in a cabin out back near the stables. With Mr. Sanford gone, I guess that means Jake is the only one you have to distract. He's most likely preparing his evening meal about now."

"I'm not going to distract him," said Fargo. "You are."

"Why am I distracting him? And while I'm distracting him, what are you going to do?"

"Where do I find Sanford's study?"

She blinked. "Why, uh, it's the room directly below this one. But what—"

Fargo growled. "I've been out of commission for close to twenty hours. That's too damn long. Something stinks, and it involves you."

She arched an eyebrow. "Well, thanks."

"I mean," he said with exaggerated patience, "that if it involves you, it's my job to root it out and put a stop to it."

She considered this briefly and nodded. "That does make sense."

"While you're keeping Jake busy, I'm going to give Sanford's study a quick going over."

"But what are you looking for?"

"I don't know. I'll know when I find it. You have

Jake set you up with a buggy to take us out of here. He'll know of Sanford's displeasure at having me here. He'll consider it his duty to accommodate you in getting me the hell off the property."

"That sounds reasonable as distractions go." She nodded to the stack of banded currency on the bedside table. "What about the money?"

"Leave it," said Fargo. "It'll serve notice to Sanford that I'm not for sale. I choose where my money comes from. In my social circle, not being for sale is a good reputation to have."

She smiled. Mona Lisa time again.

"And I'll bet you do have a reputation."

"Let's go," he said.

Another glance up and down the hallway determined that the hallway remained deserted. Fargo unholstered the Colt. He motioned for Lara to wait while he stepped with his back to the wall beside the door. He toed the door open.

Experience had taught him to always be ready for an ambush, especially in unfamiliar surroundings. Framed there in the doorway, he would have made a perfect target for a gunman placed inside the house by Sanford to take him out. Fargo didn't expect this to happen. Sanford appeared to be playing it slick, not rough, in trying to get rid of him. But Fargo had stayed alive by always making sure.

He propelled himself from the bedroom in a somersaulting roll, coming to his feet in the middle of the hall, at the head of the stairs, scanning the area around him both upstairs and downstairs to the foyer, with narrowed eyes and the Colt seeking a target.

A tomblike, echoey hush pervaded the vaulted ceilings and spacious areas of this mansion that was more like a castle than a private residence in El Paso, Texas.

Fargo motioned with his free arm. Lara joined him. He nodded down the stairs.

"Get to work."

She surprised him then, by tilting her lips up ever so slightly as she brushed by him moving toward the stairs. Her lips brushing across his cheek and the natural, lingering musky scent of her stroked his nostrils and made him smile. He stood there, admiring her backside as she continued down the stairs to disappear from his sight once she reached the foyer.

He gave her a sixty-second count, prepared to take the steps two at a time and come to her rescue at the first indication from her. Before long, he heard a screen door shut from downstairs, at the rear of the house. He waited motionless for another two minutes, which seemed like an eternity. He had never been much good at waiting. But he wanted to allot sufficient time for Lara to initiate her distraction of Jake.

When he was satisfied that sufficient time had passed, Fargo descended the stairs and moved to the door designated by Lara, situated directly beneath the upstairs bedroom they'd just vacated.

He tried to door handle. It was locked.

Fargo reached down and unsheathed his Arkansas toothpick. He wedged it between the door and the frame and worked the bolt back and forth. When he felt a catch, Fargo yanked hard on the handle and quickly slipped inside, easing the door shut behind him.

Sanford's sanctum sanctorum was a man's retreat, by God. The walls were lined with dark oak paneling, in the center of which there was an oversized portrait of G. Chadwell Sanford himself, seated, holding a cane, his swagger apparent even in portraiture, as if he owned the world. In addition to the portrait, several other oil works decorated the room. Behind him, Fargo turned to see stuffed animal heads mounted above the door, glass eyes glinting in the rays of reddish dusk sunlight slanting through arched windows. To his left, a sea of shelved books, to his right a line of file cabinets, culminating in a secretary's small work area dominated by an ornate, glass-topped desk. There was a humidor on the desk. The air in the study was redolent with the scent of fine tobacco.

Fargo scanned the walls facing the bookshelves. There was no reason to think that a man as successful as Sanford would be foolish enough to leave any sort of incriminating evidence in any place where it could be accidentally discovered, which is why he wasted no time with the desk or file cabinets.

A pastoral landscape hung crookedly against the oak paneling, as if it had been recently handled. Fargo set aside the painting and uncovered a hidden safe.

Over the years the Trailsman had pretty much seen it all. He'd picked up the skills necessary to survive as he went along. Occasionally, more than one seemingly useless talent found its way into his mental armory. Skye Fargo wasn't one for stealing, wasn't one for robbing banks either, but sometimes you just needed to know how to bust open a safe, and fortunately for Fargo, he knew exactly what to do.

After the third try, the safe's tumblers fell into place. He swung open the small cylindrical metal door and made a quick perusal of the safe's contents. He found pretty much what he expected to find. There were deeds and a stack of ledger books, each clearly marked for an individual business—The Cattleman's Western Range Group, The El Paso Builders Association, The Rio Grand Mill Works, every sort of business—and this confirmed Fargo's suspicions of the old rascal. Sanford was keeping a second, secret set of books, and the reason for that could only be that he was swindling somebody. And the only person that came to mind was Lara Newton's father, Sanford's partner in enterprise.

Fargo slowed to spend extra time examining a ledger book that had no address, no business or private name, and in which the transactions were not clearly identified, as they were in the other books. This ledger book was a thing apart, with numerically coded orders that would allow its owner to utilize it to keep track of business transactions while it was indecipherable to an unschooled eye like Fargo's.

Fargo made his best attempt to decipher the numerical coding, paging slowly through the book from front to back three times over, slower each time. It started to come together in his mind. The code became clear enough, although it provided no real answers.

The ledger was page after page of four columns of numbers recorded in a meticulous script. The first column was no mystery. Dates, going back eighteen months. The fourth column was easy. Round numbers in the upper hundreds, near a thousand—sums of money. The third column showed lower amounts, also in round numbers. This, Fargo surmised, was for whatever merchandise was being traded. Okay, simple enough. The third and fourth columns represented the quantities of goods and prices paid. The numbers in these columns repeated fairly consistently. And that left the second column as the tough nut to crack. These numbers were each five random digits, again reappearing consistently, and ofttimes matching up with the other columns.

The final deduction?

Sanford was moving some sort of merchandise to a small circle of customers. The merchandise could be goods siphoned from the legitimate enterprises, but the idea of work being carried out after business hours suggested that, more likely, something illegal was involved—contraband of some sort was being dealt in. But with numbers instead of identifiable names, and with no name or address appearing on the ledger book, this was as far as Fargo could go.

He returned the stack of ledger books and, with a dissatisfied growl, closed the safe and replaced the painting over it. The clip-clop of hooves, and the wheels of a buggy drawing to a stop on the crushed-stone driveway in front of the house drifted to him. He eased out of the study as effortlessly as he had entered, crossed the foyer, and stepped from the house onto the front porch.

A bald man, near fifty, wearing soiled dungarees and brogans, was alighting from a buggy in which Lara sat as a passenger.

A gun-metal gray spread of clouds shielded the setting sun. The breeze, sighing in from the north, was picking up a bite as the night drew near.

Fargo approached the buggy.

The bald man regarded him with a surly squint. "You must be him," he rasped. There was scar tissue around his eyes. His nose had been broken more than once, and he had cauliflower ears.

"I'm him," Fargo said. He passed Jake, swung aboard the buggy, and picked up the reins. He grinned at Lara. "Pardon the grammar, Boston."

She chuckled. "You're terrible," she said under her breath.

Jake snorted up a healthy wad of phlegm and spat. "You're also out of here," he snarled at Fargo. "Go on, beat it, trail bum. And go easy with that buggy. It's valuable."

Fargo gave the man his most pleasant smile. "You sure your boss wants me to know that? I mean, I might take this here buggy and sell it, or something."

Jake planted his feet squarely, making his oversized hands into fists. "Don't sass me. Mr. Sanford, he'll expect to know where you leave this here buggy. I fixed it up for Miss Lara, not for you, drifter. You take good care of that rig." He looked past Fargo, at Lara. "Miss, I sure hope you know what you're doing, it being dark and you taking off with a rounder like this." He returned his glare to Fargo. "This here young lady—any harm befalls her I'll track you down and kill you myself."

"No, you won't," Fargo said matter-of-factly. "But I'll tell you what, Jake. I don't have the time or the mean streak to take down an old tiger like you. But I can help you out some if you feel like lighting out and getting a new start somewhere else, with plenty of money to grubstake you."

Jake's scarred eyelids tightened. "What the blue blazes are you talking about, mister?"

"I'm talking about a stack of money," said Fargo. "I'm talking about one thousand dollars. I can put it in your pocket, within five minutes. If you had that kind of money, what would you do?"

"Are you japing me? If you're funning me, mister, I'll—"

"A thousand dollars," said Fargo. "What would you do with that kind of money?"

Fargo felt Lara rest a hand on his arm. "Skye, you're talking about the money Mr. Sanford left for you?"

Fargo nodded. "Reckon that's as good as telling me

I can do what I want with it. What do you say, Jake? What would you do with a thousand dollars to spend?"

"Reckon I'd head on home to Arkansas," said Jake. "Get me a piece of land. Get me a woman."

Lara leaned forward to speak past Fargo. "You may have Mr. Sanford's people coming after you."

"Anyone coming after me will get only as close as I want them to," Jake assured her. "Give me a thousand dollars to hold on to, and they'll be dead or bleeding." He added, "I could have taken you just now, son, if you'd have pushed it."

Fargo's grin was back to being pleasant. "You know something, Jake? I half believe that. I surely do. Now back to business. Do you want to earn that thousand dollars?"

"What do I got to do?"

"I want to know where I can find Sanford. When he left, he told me he was on his way to a business meeting."

Jake rubbed the back of his red neck with one of his ham-sized hands. "I don't know nothing about no meeting. He might have been just trying to impress you. You want to know the truth of the business, this here Sanford's sort of a first-class horse's ass." Jake seemed to realize what he'd just said, and bowed in Lara's direction, a strangely gallant gesture. "Begging your pardon, ma'am." Then his eyes got serious again. "This here Sanford's up to some underhanded business down at the Texas Metal Works. That's where he went off to. It's a big factory just south of the tracks on the main stretch the other side of town. I don't know what it is that he's up to down there exactly, but that's where I took him one or twice when he was too lazy to take himself. Sanford, he thinks he owns me because he pays me enough to have me call him sir." Jake spat again, then looked at Lara. "Sorry, ma'am."

Fargo said, "The money's banded and on the bedside table up in the bedroom where they had me."

"I know the one."

"The money's yours. Good luck to you, Jake."

"And to you, drifter."

Fargo snapped the reins. Lara sent Jake a farewell wave, which Jake returned. Then the horse drew the buggy onto the driveway leading away from the house. As they jounced along, Fargo found himself to be the subject of bemused scrutiny by the woman beside him.

"You," said Lara, "are the most spontaneous, rough-hewn, amazing man I have ever encountered."

Fargo reined their horse onto the road leading to El Paso, leaving the property.

He handed the reins to Lara. "Here, take these," he requested.

She did so, quite efficiently. "I don't mean to be a nosy woman," she said, after they'd traveled a half mile, "but where the hell are we going?"

"Thought you knew."

"We're on our way to the Texas Metal Works factory."

"I'm gong to find out what Sanford is up to," said Fargo. "I want to see if it has anything to do with your brother."

"*We're* going to find out," she said.

"I work best alone," said Fargo.

"Yes, but this time you're working for me."

Lara snapped the reins, and the buggy picked up speed, heading into town.

# 5

The Texas Metal Works was set on four acres surrounded by a ten-foot-high brick wall. There was a closed, wrought-iron gate facing the main road, which was poorly lit. It was surrounded by mostly similar industrial sites that were shut down at this hour. It was an isolated part of town.

The daytime breeze had picked up to a brisk, cold night wind. The lights of El Paso, not far behind them beyond the railroad tracks, muted the starlight.

Fargo held the buggy's reins. He and Lara rode past the main gate once so he could get a glance inside. He saw a gatehouse just inside the main gate. A night watchman could be seen reading a dime novel, his feet propped up on a desk, and a visor cap pushed back on his head.

*Good*, thought Fargo. *Lax security.*

Or was that just a front? Sanford seemed fond of keeping up false fronts.

At the far end of the brick wall, Fargo jerked the reins, directing their horse—a trustworthy gray mare—off the road. They traveled along the wall for twenty yards, to where the shadows became almost complete darkness, well removed from the distant illumination of scanty street lighting.

Fargo tugged the reins and the mare pulled to a stop beneath a tall oak tree that blotted out the starlight and made the shadows darkest along the base of the wall.

The wall blocked the wind. The air wasn't so cold. A night owl hooted from the woods surrounding the Metal Works.

"Now what?" asked Lara.

"Now you make sure that no one messes with this buggy, because we may need to hotfoot it out of here right smart."

"You mean you go in and I stay out here on my what-you-call-it." There was determination in her voice. "Uh-uh, Fargo. I don't think so."

"Well, I do," said Fargo. He set down the reins. "You're paying me to do what I can to help you find your brother. That's my understanding of our agreement, anyway."

"What's your point?" Her tone was snippy.

"Let me earn my money," said Fargo. "If I'm not back in fifteen minutes, get this buggy the hell back to Sanford's place and act like you don't know a thing."

"That shouldn't be too difficult," she said waspishly.

He left the buggy, using its added height to easily make a small leap that allowed him to grasp an overhanging tree branch with both hands. He hoisted himself up, close to the trunk of the mighty oak. Another modest leap brought him atop the two-foot-wide wall. He pressed his body flat to the brick and mortar and reconnoitered the factory grounds from his vantage point.

He couldn't see the main gate or the gatehouse from his position. The factory grounds were, for the most part, cloaked in darkness. He saw a structure that looked like an office building set against the inside of the front wall. There were scrap heaps as well as carefully tiered and sheltered rows of steel rail, and a large building with smokestacks that was oddly quiet and dark. There were wagons here and there, but no sign of a stable or any sign of habitation.

Fargo had neglected to ask Jake if the Texas Metal Works was operational or shut down. The latter seemed to be the case.

He left his perch in an easy drop that landed him well behind the wall, well inside the factory grounds. He ran to the seemingly vacant main building and pressed his back to its wall. He unleathered the Colt and eased his way cautiously along the wall, toward the rear of the building. He had already ascertained, from initial reconnoitering, that there was no activity visible from the front of this building, which faced the main gate. Sanford was too smart for that. And sure enough, he found plenty going on when he looked around the rear corner of the building.

There was a loading dock. Three mule-team wagons were pulled up to the dock, and two men per wagon were unloading crates from the wagons, transferring the crates into the warehouse. They were hard-looking men, with the low-slung-pistol look of gunslingers. There was a window ten feet above Fargo's head, no doubt designed to maximize daylight to illuminate the building's interior. Lighting from inside was visible, making the windowpane appear as a roseate pair of eyes.

He made quick work of a discarded wagon, from which he jumped to grab hold of a nearby tree. Fargo scaled the tree's branches to the lighted window on his left, like a pirate boarding a Spanish galleon. He positioned himself close enough to the widow to press an eye to the glass.

He had a bird's-eye view of the loading dock. The

last of the crates were being transported through a doorway in the wall fronting the dock. That room would be second of these two windows, Fargo decided.

After the last of the crates had been carried through, and the gunslingers had returned to their wagons, G. Chadwell Sanford closed and locked the door.

The man with Sanford wore civilian clothes, but had about him the bearing of a military officer. He might as well have been wearing a uniform. A *rogue officer*, thought Fargo.

He was starting to get an idea of what this could be about.

As he watched, Sanford produced a fat packet from inside his coat and handed the packet to the man, who examined its contents, nodded his satisfaction, and pocketed the packet inside his overcoat.

A deal had just been concluded. A military officer, diverting Government Issue to Sanford for a tidy profit.

Fargo edged himself in the direction of the second window. It was dimmer inside this vast storeroom, but there was enough light for him to see the rectangular crates that had been carried in here and stacked row upon row.

Rifles. Sanford could be dealing in nothing else. Even an idiot would know what was in those tiered crates, and Fargo—except for when it came to women—was no idiot.

Thousands of rifles, he estimated. Neatly ordered rows of thousands of rifles ready to be sold to the anonymous buyers in Sanford's coded ledger.

Fargo felt himself slipping. He lost his hold of the mortar ridge surrounding the window, and when his fingers let go and with nowhere for his boots to find a toehold, he naturally fell backwards into space.

He dropped like a sack of grain. He landed in the bed of the empty wagon with a thud loud enough to be heard in downtown El Paso.

It wouldn't have been so bad but for the pain he'd been keeping under wraps from his earlier wounds, which had increased due to the physical exertion of climbing trees and scaling walls. The wind was knocked out of his lungs with a powerful poof and raw, flaming agony scraped his bare nerve ends and made the world blur and spin around him, thankfully only momentarily.

He sat up and shook his head to clear it. The pain again receded. The world stopped leaning. He'd held on to the Colt.

He started to stand, to jump from the wagon. He paused when he realized that four gunmen stood in a semicircle around the wagon, each holding a rifle aimed at him. That left two unaccounted for.

Sanford stepped through their ranks to stand staring at where Fargo stood in the wagon. He held a lantern. In its eerie golden glow, Sanford looked anything but cherubic. His eyes were like black marbles in jowly folds of flesh, no longer cheery, but mean and dangerous, predatory, calculating.

"Well, well, Mr. Fargo. What a surprise."

Fargo lowered his Colt. "Howdy there, Sanford."

Sanford chuckled. Not a pleasant sound. "My dear, dear man, you are a most audacious fellow, I must say."

"That shot to the head last night must have rattled my brains," said Fargo.

"I beg you, sir. Drop the pistol, or I shall find myself compelled to order you promptly dispatched."

"Reckon that's clear enough fancy talk for me," said Fargo. He tossed down his Colt, making certain that it landed not in the wagon but upon the ground beside the wagon.

Sanford nodded. "Very good. And now may I inquire as to what the hell you are doing here, Mr. Fargo?"

"What if I don't feel like telling you, Mr. Sanford?"

Sanford snarled. "I am not amused by levity. How do you happen to be here? Is my niece involved?"

Fargo stayed standing in the wagon.

"She's not your niece, dammit. Stop pretending she is. Let's talk about you and me tonight."

"I am," said Sanford. "Now then, sir, please raise your arms so I may see your hands. I understand from eyewitness reports on that train last night that you're rather handy with a boot knife. A hat full of tricks, as it were."

Fargo raised his hands. As a matter of fact, he'd taken recent possession of a straight-edged razor that he'd stashed beneath the inside of his hatband. Unfortunately, he couldn't see where that would do him much good here, staring down the barrels of the rifles aimed at him. But he had long ago learned that if you could keep your opponent engaged in conversation, as he was doing with Sanford, you stood a chance of creating that break, that one opening, to get the slightest edge and make a try at getting out alive.

"Guess I'm wondering why I'm being granted the pleasure of this conversation, and not just getting shot full of holes by your boys."

"Simple, really," said Sanford. "I need to know what you know. I need to know who you really are, and why you've been sticking your beak into my business. Who sent you? Is Lara involved? Are you working for her or her father? You see? I must back-track and take precautions. We have agreed to be plainspoken, you and I, have we not, sir?"

"You sure do talk a lot," said Fargo. "I'm suppos-ing that Lara's father, your dear old best friend, doesn't have the slightest idea that you're an arms supplier. Damn your soul, Sanford. The West is going to be peaceful someday, but not as long as men like you, who deal in death, are allowed to go unchecked."

Sanford's brow furrowed. "Are you with a govern-ment agency? Were you sent to investigate me?"

"Let's trade information," said Fargo. "You know something about me. What about you? What tribes are you selling guns to?"

Sanford regarded Fargo with open admiration in the lantern's golden glow. "I repeat, sir, you are the most audacious fellow I have ever met. Well, to an-swer your question, I am only selling guns to the tribes to be used however they see fit."

Fargo felt a facial tic tighten his squint into a gri-mace. "They're using those rifles to wage war on set-tlers, and you know it."

Sanford shrugged. "The tribes also happen to wage war on each other, as they have for hundreds of years, I've been told." He smirked. "So maybe in their wars of attrition against each other I am indirectly thinning their ranks and benefitting our great nation's west-ward expansion. No matter to me. I'm a businessman. And by the way, the tribes aren't my only customers."

Fargo nodded. "I expect there would be any num-ber of scoundrels willing to pay good money for rifles diverted from the Army. That's one of the reasons they put Fort Survival out there—because of those marauding gangs."

"And so it is again your turn to answer some questions in this verbal joust between us, Mr. Fargo. Who are you working for? How much information have you learned, and to whom have you reported it? You can tell me quickly, and die quickly. Or my men have ways to make you talk—ways with a knife, that will make you tell me everything and then beg to die. So tell me, Fargo, and let us be done with this unpleasant business. What do you say?"

Before Fargo could answer, there was a commotion from around the side of the building. To his right came the remaining two gunslingers, each with a hold of one of Lara's arms.

She was struggling to no avail. There was no sign of her gun-toting purse.

The furrows in Sanford's brow deepened. "What have we here?"

Fargo sighed. "We have a headstrong female who won't listen to orders."

# 6

As the gunmen led Lara to where Sanford stood, she ceased physically resisting. She glanced up at Fargo in the wagon.

"Secure the buggy," she said. "What the hell kind of an order is that? I didn't travel this far from Boston to secure buggies."

One of the gunslingers holding her told Sanford, "We caught her scaling the wall on the far side of the foundry. I'd say she was taking the same route he took to get in." He nodded to Fargo.

Fargo could only shake his head. "Lara," he said.

"Ah, yes, Lara." Oiliness oozed from Sanford's smile. "This does beg a question, does it not? Why precisely *have* you traveled west, my dear?"

Lara assumed that ramrod-straight posture of hers. "I have nothing to say to you."

Sanford snickered, and the unclean sound chilled Fargo's blood.

"Oh, you poor, self-deluded innocent, wanting to believe that you are so strong."

"Strong enough," Lara snapped. "Try me."

"Lara," Fargo said again, caution in his voice.

Sanford said, "I was just telling Fargo here how a man with a knife could make him scream out everything I want to know, and then he would beg to die." Sanford stepped up to her suddenly. He pawed one of her breasts, squeezing it roughly. He smiled when she cried out in pain. He said, "It's even easier to torture the truth from a woman, my dear."

One of the gunmen snickered. "And a hell of a lot more fun."

"As for you, Mr. Fargo," he said with a sarcastic sneer, "I think that, having Miss Newton as we do, we consequently have no need of *you*."

"What's the plan?" asked Fargo, still playing for time, still looking for that edge, even though he knew his time was running out. "Are you going to tell Lara's father that she just up and disappeared, the way her brother dropped out of sight?"

"I had nothing to do with that," said Sanford. "That's a military matter."

"Maybe," said Fargo. In all the excitement, he had managed to lower his arms without anyone noticing or saying anything.

Lara took a threatening step toward Sanford, only to be further restrained by the gunmen who held her. Her eyes were filled with revulsion. "You had something to do with Jeffrey's disappearance?"

"I had nothing to do with poor Jeffery's disappearance," said Sanford, "but I will have everything to do with your demise."

He turned to the four gunslingers lined up to his left, their rifles still poised and ready for action. Sanford started to snarl a command.

In that final moment, when it looked like there would be no lucky break, Fargo found himself making eye contact with Lara.

She gave him a rock-steady stare that seemed to say, *I know what I'm doing. Trust me, and here's the break you've been waiting for.*

She cried out, "Oh my God, please don't let him die! *No!*"

She appeared to lose consciousness, and collapsed where she stood between the two gunslingers who held her by her arms, her falling body tilting each of them sideways, off-balance, completely unprepared.

Sanford's jaw dropped before his order to fire could be voiced, so distracted was he by the sight of the woman fainting.

Fargo used this diversion to vault from the wagon even as the riflemen regained their focus, opening fire without waiting to be told. Their bullets spattered off the foundry wall behind where Fargo had been standing an eye blink before. But he was already flat on the ground where he had dropped the Colt. His fingers grasped the pistol and he brought it up on the line of four riflemen who were lowering their aim at him . . . but not fast enough.

The Colt barked four times in rapid succession. The four riflemen were knocked off their feet into dead sprawls, the rifles flying from their lifeless fingers.

The men who had been occupied with Lara reacted as quickly as they could, letting her fall, each clawing for their holstered sidearms. The Colt spoke twice more and the final two gunmen toppled to the dust.

Lara dashed toward Fargo.

Fargo went into a crouch. He snapped open the cylinder of the Colt and, with a sharp, one-handed gesture, shook loose the six spent shells, reaching with his other hand for fresh bullets from his cartridge belt.

Sanford stepped back a pace. His jaw remained dropped, this time in utter amazement at the rapidity with which Fargo had just killed all of his men. But it only took an instant for that realization to twist Sanford's face into an unrecognizable mask of rage and determination. For a second, Fargo saw the ferocity that must have been there when he was a young man, buried over the years but resurfacing now with a vengeance.

Sanford threw aside the lantern. He dived for one of the dead men's dropped rifles. The lantern smashed and spilled kerosene that torched immediately, illuminating Sanford as he brought the rifle up on Fargo with the speed of a man half his age.

The firelight illuminated Fargo, too, as he crouched there, slapping the Colt's cylinder shut as the rifle drew a bead on him.

Lara dew up short, not going to Fargo as she'd intended, thus allowing him a fuller range of movement now that she was out of the kill zone.

Fargo dived to the ground as Sanford bellowed like an enraged beast and fired at where Fargo had just been.

There came the high-pitched, keening whistle sound of a ricochet, then another, as the powerful velocity of the bullet pinged and whistled from the wall to the ground and then off at an angle into space.

From his prone position, Fargo aimed the Colt at Sanford, but held his fire.

In the firelight from the spilt kerosene, Sanford could clearly be seen sitting amid the sprawled bodies of his men as if considering the matter a moment more before deciding to plop down upon his back and join them.

Fargo got slowly to his feet.

Lara ran up to him. She looked at Sanford, and averted her eyes. "Oh, my God."

The upper left quarter of Sanford's face was missing, replaced by a gaping hole that looked as if it was

57

filled with pulped tomato that reflected the flames rising near the wagon.

"Ricochet," said Fargo. "A heavy-caliber rifle bullet still has plenty of punch after only two. Uncle Sanford blew his own brains out."

"It looks like he's also torched the Texas Metal Works," she observed.

The wagon behind them had become consumed in flames that were now eating at, and igniting, the dry timber of the foundry building.

"Tell you what," said Fargo. "It might not be a bad idea for us to hightail it out of here right about now."

"Well, lead the way."

"Great," he grumbled. "*Now* you take orders like nobody's business. All right. Let's go this way."

As they withdrew, a man was calling tentatively from the far corner of the building; that would be the night watchman from the gatehouse who had no doubt been instructed by Sanford to stay away, keep people out, and not pay attention to anything while Sanford transacted his secret dirty business. But gunplay and fire had drawn his attention.

Fargo led Lara to a side gate at the rear of the grounds, well removed from the foundry, which was becoming rapidly engulfed in flames.

The night watchman could be seen wandering about in a daze amid the sea of bodies while the fire raged.

Fargo assisted Lara up and over the surrounding wall and then scaled it himself. They raced along the base of the brick wall and moments later they reached the buggy. The mare was contentedly munching tall grass.

"Ah," said Lara as they boarded the buggy. "Secure as I left it." She was out of breath.

Fargo felt the same, but didn't let it show. "Don't be fresh. We're not out of this yet."

The cloudy night sky rippled with the reflected angry reds and golden hues of the fire. The clanging of a volunteer bucket brigade bell could be heard in the distance.

At the end of the wall, Fargo reined the buggy onto the main road and steered them back toward the center of El Paso.

They rode out of El Paso an hour later. It felt good to be on the trail again. Lara had found a spirited dun, while Fargo rode his impressive Ovaro stallion, a tall black-and-white paint with distinctive markings.

After leaving the foundry, they'd headed straight to the stable where he'd roused a sleepy-eyed, grumpy old attendant.

The old geezer had been won over quickly enough in equal parts by Lara's beauty and charm, and some extra *dinero* Fargo slipped him—not to mention Fargo's setting up the sale of a horse to Lara. The attendant would no doubt take his own bite of the sale price before paying off the owner. He told them that the owner had found the dun too spirited, more trouble than it was worth, and it had been for sale but had a reputation in this country, so no one had yet to come forward to buy it. So Lara bought it, after Fargo getting the geezer to knock down the price some more by offering the buggy to sweeten the deal. Jake had been right. The buggy was valuable merchandise, and G. Chadwell Sanford would certainly have no further use for it.

By the time the deal was concluded, Lara had the big dun in love with her—literally eating out of her hand, lapping its tongue at the sugar cubes she offered as she stroked its mane and whispered things Fargo could not hear. Fargo couldn't be sure, but the horse seemed to be actually smiling.

They each filled one saddlebag with grain and another with some dried fruit, which the attendant fetched for another healthy tip, and they were on their way, galloping out of El Paso.

Fargo had been through many an adventure, and some damn close calls, with the giant, graceful, fearless Ovaro, which lengthened its stride once they began to shake loose the shackles of civilization. Horse and man shared a sense of liberation from the confines of trains and rooms and streets, needing the open trail that stretched across this prairie like the body needs water.

For a lady from Boston, Lara was a damn good rider. She rode Western style, leaning forward in the saddle, urging her steed to match, side by side, the flat-out pace set by the Ovaro. She rode abreast of Fargo, her laughter a beautiful thing even though mostly lost because of galloping hooves. The wind whipped her hair, loosening and untaming blond tresses that bounced on her shoulders in the starlight.

They rode on, fast and hard, following a ruler-straight, but seldom-used trail that tracked into the night, leaving El Paso far behind. They slowed down eventually.

Fargo set a steady but not strenuous pace, northward. There was a set determination to his posture, and to the pace he set, which Lara matched. Several miles beyond town, he reined east when the trail met a fork in the road, and before long they had passed through the sleepy, outlying hamlets.

The open prairie, beneath a clearing sky of sparkling stars, belonged to them. They maintained a steady pace, encountering no one at this time of night. Scant conversation passed between them. The night wind was harsh out here in the open, and it needled at their exposed flesh. They hunched in their saddles against the cold as they rode on.

Dawn was etching a thin strip of silver along the flat horizon to the east when they drew up in a draw, forming a natural windbreak.

"We'll be riding into the fort after morning formation," said Fargo. "I'll want to speak with Colonel Talbot and get started on the matter of your brother as soon as possible after we arrive there."

They were the first words they'd exchanged in more than an hour of riding.

"Right now and right here is a good time and place to rest up for the ride in."

Fargo liked the quickness with which she picked up on things in this new world of the West that she was opening herself up to. She may have been uppercrust Eastern money, and he'd always had an automatic distrust of those of that class, but everyone in the West came from somewhere else, and if people were to be judged on their merits, not their pasts . . . well, she was all right.

They unsaddled their mounts, attaching nosebags of grain so the Ovaro and the dun could enjoy a well-earned repast of their own. The horses were funny, the dun and the Ovaro tolerating each other's presence out of deference to their masters, but standing side by side, facing in opposite directions as they chomped from their feedbags.

As dawn came on, the wind died down, Fargo and Lara were just withdrawing foodstuff from their saddlebags.

As she munched, Lara said with mild sarcasm, "Looks like we found ourselves shelter just in time."

"West Texas," said Fargo, washing down a mouthful with a drink from his canteen. "It'll be hotter than blazes come noon."

After eating, they stretched out for a short rest.

When Fargo opened his eyes to sunlight a short time later, he felt refreshed, ready to continue. It was a trick a man had to master if he expected to survive in a hostile environment. He had long ago learned to catch catnaps whenever he could afford them, such as he did now, to restore his energy and keep his survival instincts sharp. It felt blissful to be stroked by the day's first, soft sunlight.

Then the pleasant feeling increased when he became aware that, sometime during the catnap, Lara had gone from lying alongside him to curling up in his arms, snuggled in with her head on his chest, sound asleep, her tousled blond hair under his nostrils.

The ball of the sun had barely shown a third of itself above the tabletop-flat horizon, but the cold of the night was already yielding to the warming of the sunrise. Wispy saffron clouds gilded a gray sky that was quickly turning blue.

Fargo woke the woman in his arms by shifting his shoulder ever so slightly. She awoke to yawn and rub her eyes with two loosely balled fists, like a kid. He shifted into a sitting position, easing her into the same.

"Good morning," he said, hoping for the best.

He had also long ago learned that every woman had her own way of waking up, and even the sweetest flower of womanhood could be downright squirrelly, if that was her nature, upon awaking. He sighed with some relief when she popped to her feet with pep.

Facing away from him, she stretched a wide-armed stretch, catching the full effect of the rising sun.

"What a beautiful new day, Skye."

Watching her stand there in her heavy jacket, riding britches, and boots, her loose hair flowing free, attractively tangled by sleep, was enough to wake up Fargo. Hell, it was a sight to awaken a dead man! She was a fine figure of a woman, and Fargo wondered if he hadn't been a damned fool not to have taken the time to have her—all the way, as she'd wanted—the day before in a bedroom of the Sanford mansion . . . or right now, for that matter. His eyes traveled over the fine-lined curves of her figure and her attractive, tight backside beneath those clinging britches. He could tug her by the arm right now, pull her down, and have a mighty fine time with her, and Lara would have plenty of fun too. But for the moment, he had other needs to tend to. He banished all thoughts of Lara and the things he'd like to do to her from his head, and got to his feet.

The bandage around his head had loosened during the night of hard riding and his snooze upon the ground. He tugged the gauze away and touched gingerly around the bullet graze. Sore, but he'd survive the wound.

They saddled their horses and prepared to break this temporary camp.

"You know," Lara said, "I've been thinking, Skye."

Fargo was tightening the cinch of his saddle. "Is that a good thing?" he asked innocently.

She ignored him. "I'm still not sure I understand exactly what happened last night with Uncle . . . with Mr. Sanford. I mean, don't you think I have a right to have it explained to me, since I *am* involved and I *am* paying the freight?"

"You keep reminding me of that." Fargo straightened from cinching the saddle. He checked to secure his saddlebags and the rifle scabbard for his Henry rifle. Then he swung into the saddle. "All right, here's your morning report, Boss. Yes, Sanford was behind the attempted abduction of you on the train the other night."

"Because he was selling rifles diverted from the military?"

Fargo shrugged. "I'm only guessing at the relevant details, but here goes. Sanford was using his and your father's business concerns to cover that arms business, and I'll wager he was skimming more than his share from their other partnership profits. Sanford had to make sure you wouldn't find out about it. Maybe he was planning to have those outlaws hold you for ransom from your father back East, then kill you."

"But what about my brother? Do you think Jeffrey learned about Sanford's arms business? As a soldier, Jeff would be obligated to act."

Fargo centered his vision on a fixed point on the western horizon, which was still enshrouded with the purple shadows of sage.

"If he was a good soldier."

She swung toward him in her saddle. "He was. And if Sanford was involved in Jeff's disappearance, it was because Jeff found out something about Sanford that got Jeff killed. What do you think, Skye? I came all this distance for answers. Do you think Sanford was involved with Jeff's disappearance?"

"In a word, maybe," said Fargo. "Last night at the factory, Sanford told us that he wasn't involved in whatever happened to Jeff."

Lara snorted. "Of course he'd say that."

Fargo stared at the fixed point where shadows on the horizon were gradually dissipating.

"Not necessarily," he said. "Last night Sanford held all the cards when he denied his involvement. I had rifles trained on me and his boys had hold of you."

"I'm trying to forget that."

"My point," said Fargo, "is that when he denied involvement Sanford had no reason to lie. He expected to kill us both. Maybe he was involved, but not directly. The trail goes farther, and we're on it."

She became aware of his intense staring toward the horizon. She followed his gaze.

"What are you looking at?"

"Don't you see them?"

"No, I . . . oh, my God!"

From this distance it was difficult to tell for sure, but he counted five braves on ponies, dressed in full warrior gear. They had become starkly highlighted in sunrays that swept across the terrain from the east as the sun fully rose above the horizon.

The braves were on a ridge, approximately a quarter mile away. They made no attempt to advance or withdraw.

"They could have been tracking us some last night," said Fargo.

With a press of his knees, he commanded the Ovaro, and the horse made the easy climb out of the draw, returning to the rocky but level ground.

Lara leaned forward the whispered to the dun. Her horse again kept pace with the Ovaro. She and Fargo rode side by side when they regained the trail.

In the distance, the mounted braves remained stationary, not following.

Lara called over to Fargo as they rode.

"Are they going to cause us trouble?"

"If that was their intention," Fargo called back, "we'd already have our hands full." Another press of his knees and the Ovaro stretched into a ground-covering gallop, and again Lara kept apace. "Come on," said Fargo. "Let's give those braves something to look at. We're riding to Fort Survival."

# 7

It was a standard layout for a frontier military out-post, situated on high ground with clear visual command of the surrounding terrain, a thoroughly defensible position comprised of barracks, a parade ground, administration buildings, and other structures, all within the confines of a twenty-foot high wall of pine, cut from trees hauled a considerable distance from the mountain forests. Atop one of the four corner watchtowers, an American flag unfurled in a warm breeze. A sign over the open main gate read FORT SURVIVAL.

Fargo and Lara rode up the wide, well-trodden approach trail to the fort. There had been no more sightings of Indian war parties tracking them.

The sun was at its midmorning point in a blue sky, and the temperature was rising steadily. The day wasn't quite hot yet, but soon would be.

There was a scattering of teepees to one side of the front gate, just outside the wall—living accommodations for the Indian scouts and their families, and other "friendlies" who provided services, a common practice in outposts like this where soldiers hired so-called "friendly Indians" for lowly tasks like latrine duty and cleaning stables.

Fargo and Lara rode, side by side, with a nod to the sentries, through the main gate into the busy fort.

Within minutes, they were shown into Colonel Talbot's office.

The office furnishings were Spartan and functional. Maps were spread across a conference table. A flag on one wall faced a portrait of the president on another, and there was not much else except for a cluttered desk.

The commanding officer of Fort Survival was a compactly built man of fifty-some years. He was muscular, and his skin, a natural mahogany color from years on the plains, was contrasted by a closely cropped, snow-white mustache.

Talbot rose from behind the desk. He was erect of statue and flat of stomach, every inch the career military man. He came around the desk with a smile as an orderly showed Fargo and Lara in.

"Well, I'll be damned." He pumped Fargo's hand with both of his own. "If it isn't Skye Fargo." Then he caught himself. "Er, my apologies, miss. I'm afraid I may have been stationed on the frontier for so long, I've come to neglect my social skills in the presence of a lady."

Lara chuckled. "That's all right, Colonel. I'm becoming accustomed to vulgarity—that is to say, the Western manner of expression. I'm Lara Newton." She smiled disarmingly.

Talbot smiled a fatherly smile. "You are Lieutenant Newton's sister?"

"Yes, sir."

"Then we have much to discuss." Talbot still clasped Fargo's hand in a hearty handshake, and rested a hand on Fargo's shoulder. "Please do forgive the coarseness of fighting men who have taken fire together. And you, Skye, how have you been?"

"Getting along, Colonel. Good to see this command

serving under the right man. Things looked right smart when we rode in."

Talbot sighed, and lost some of his good humor.

"I'm afraid, in that case, that looks can be deceiving." He gestured Lara to one of a pair of wooden armchairs facing his desk, holding the chair for her in a courtly fashion. "Please, Miss Newton, have a seat."

"Thank you, Colonel."

She lighted upon the chair not as a woman who had ridden a dun across the prairie through the night, but with the grace of a Boston lady, thought Fargo.

Talbot returned to the chair behind the desk.

"Go ahead, Skye. Take a load off. I'm interested to hear how you've come to be here with Miss Newton."

Fargo crossed to a window and stared out.

"I'll stand if it's all the same to you, sir."

Talbot chuckled. "Same old Skye."

"Reckon so," said Fargo. "Never did much cotton to passing time indoors. I'd rather we all got to jawing about why we're here."

Talbot leaned back in his chair and favored Lara with a conspiratorial grin.

"You may not know it, miss, but some time ago, Fargo here served as a scout under my command."

Fargo grumbled discontent from deep in his throat. "If you don't mind, Colonel, I'd rather we didn't discuss that."

"Then we won't," said Talbot, though he continued to smile slyly at Lara, "except to say that it involved a certain scout saving the life of a particular commanding officer."

For Fargo, the colonel didn't have to say any more.

Although he stood staring out at soldiers, civilians, and "friendlies" going about their business beyond the office window, he felt more like he was staring into some sort of magic screen that allowed him to see into the past, and the past washed through his mind.

*Bodies and bullets shouting and death screams and gunfire were everywhere.*

*The soldier next to Fargo caught an arrow right through the left eye, the arrowhead piercing his brain, the arrow protruding from the man's head as he was flung onto his side.*

*They'd shot Fargo's Army horse out from under him, and he was using the mount for cover. He was clustered with the half dozen surviving soldiers, all of them vigorously returning fire from a prone defensive half-circle under a copse of cottonwoods.*

*A Ute brave had revealed his position up on the high formation of boulders to fire the arrow that killed the soldier next to Fargo. Fargo took quick aim. The mighty Henry added to the blazing gunfire, and he saw the brave tumble from the rocks, behind which at least twenty other braves were hurling down a barrage of arrows and bullets upon the trapped soldiers and their scout.*

*Fargo stayed low behind his dead mount. He lever-actioned another round into the chamber and brought his eyes back to where Colonel Talbot lay sprawled in a clearing about twenty feet away, beside his own dead horse. There was an arrow sticking out of Talbot's shoulder.*

*The ambush had been perfectly orchestrated, taking out the commanding officer first, thus disrupting the chain of command from the top, adding to the chaos of attack.*

*At first Fargo thought Talbot was dead. Then he saw Talbot prop himself on one knee and clasp the arrow with his good hand. Talbot gave a tug, attempting to extract the arrow, but the effort was obviously too much for him. He cried out in pain, and fell onto his back. Dead troopers and* their horses surrounded him. He appeared to be the only one alive in the clearing.

Captain Grey was crouched behind a juniper tree, near Fargo.

He called out, "I'm coming to get you, Colonel."

Talbot lifted his head. "No, Captain! You're needed to command!"

Grey flung aside his rifle and snapped a glance at Fargo and the young troopers.

"Cover me."

He sprinted from cover.

The Utes immediately concentrated their rifle fire on him. Bullets hit the ground near Grey's feet as he ran, dodging, in Talbot's direction.

Fargo spotted one on the rocks. He picked the man off, and levered another round into the Henry. He saw another Ute, and shot him too.

Around him, the young troopers were returning fire. But these were young men, barely more than kids, and they were frightened by the accuracy of their unseen, deadly enemy. For the most part their shooting was terrible, their return fire ineffectual.

Just as he was approaching Talbot, a deadly arrow pierced Captain Grey through the neck. He stumbled and then became another dead man in the clearing.

The gunfire ceased from the rocks.

Fargo glared at the young soldiers. "Hold your fire," he commanded.

They obeyed.

The silence that followed the killing of Captain Grey held for more than a minute, and Fargo felt restless energy boiling up in his gut. Talbot lay motionless, the arrow sticking straight up from his shoulder.

One of the soldiers asked, "Why ain't nothing happening?" in a quavery, frightened whisper.

"They're fixing to surround us," said another, "and wipe us out."

Fargo made a stern shush sound. "They're happy with where they've got us for now," Fargo told the pasty-white faces of the scared young troopers to either side of him.

"What're they going to do?" a trooper asked.

"I don't aim to wait long enough to find out," said Fargo, and he lifted his voice to call across the clearing, but not loud enough for the Utes to hear. "Colonel, you still with us?"

Talbot again propped himself on his elbow. "You could call it that. But I won't be for long."

Fargo had already caught the movement, at the far side of the clearing. He saw what Talbot was referring to.

Three braves were openly stalking forward from their positions of cover, making no attempt at stealth. They were formidable, clad in moccasin boots, fringed leggings, and full war-party regalia. Two of them held rifles.

The one in the center strode with a tangible air of command, his stern visage bisected by a long-healed, shiny knife scar that ran diagonally across one eye, from his left temple to the opposite side of his jaw. This one's eyes glared like burning coals, he was clearly their leader. He held a knife, a wide-bladed Bowie surely stolen from the corpse of a soldier.

Fargo stood from behind the cover of his slain horse.

Talbot seemed to read his mind.

"Scout, no! What's left of my men . . . they need you."

"So do you, Colonel."

He tossed aside the Henry.

"Dammit, scout," Talbot barked, "I'm issuing you a direct order to stay under cover and—"

"You can't order me around, Colonel," said Fargo. "You keep forgetting that I'm a civilian. I do what I want."

**71**

After observing Fargo for a moment, the incoming braves turned and swung their rifles toward him.

Fargo's gun hand flashed and filled with the Colt. He fanned two unerring rounds, one for each of the braves, knocking them dead onto their backs.

The Ute leader paused where he stood.

Talbot looked semiconscious from loss of blood. He flopped onto his back and watched an eagle swoop gracefully, high above.

"Now boys, don't fight over me."

"You stay out of this, Colonel," said Fargo.

"Well I'll be gone to hell," Talbot muttered.

"I'm trying to prevent that," said Fargo.

Without warning, the Ute leapt at Fargo. The Ute sailed over Colonel Talbot and plowed into Fargo, the wide blade of his knife glinting in the sunshine. His shout, which bounced between the boulder formations forming the clearing, was like the growl of a predatory, wild beast descending on its prey, drunk on blood lust.

Fargo deflected the knife thrust even as the impact of the body blow sent him tumbling to the dust with his adversary atop him, a raging, muscular panther raising his arm to plunge the knife down at him. Fargo grabbed the wrist of the hand holding the knife with both of his hands, staying the blade tip an inch from his heart. He drew his knees up to his chest and kicked out with enough power to send the Ute ass over end.

Fargo was on the Ute in a heartbeat, to the sound of ribs cracking. Fargo used his left hand to grip the wrist of the man's knife hand. He smashed the wrist down against a piece of jagged rock. The wrist bone snapped, broken like a twig. Fargo seized the knife handle and tugged. He stood up and slashed downward with a single motion.

The blade of the Bowie knife severed the brave's jugular vein.

72

Fargo stepped back, avoiding the shooting burst of blood that spewed from the wound.

"They're retreating," gasped a cavalryman from where the remnants of their unit remained crouched behind their scant cover.

After watching their leader slain so brutally, a line of Utes could be glimpsed fording the river, riding single file away from the boulder formations.

Talbot was being supported in a sitting position by two of his troopers, the arrow protruding from his shoulder.

"Damn, scout, if you aren't the stubbornest son of a bitch I ever did see."

"Thanks for the compliment, sir," said Fargo. "Since we couldn't kill them all, and since they were fixing to kill us, it just made sense to kill the one of them that made the difference."

Talbot snorted, regarding Fargo keenly. "Simple as that, eh? Thank you for saving my life."

A soldier was placing the blade of an army knife to the base of the protruding arrow.

Fargo rested a hand on the trooper's shoulder.

"Hold on there. What are you doing?"

The soldier hesitated. He looked up.

"Why I'm going to cut off the arrow, sir. Our field medic is with the other column. He can remove the arrowhead when we rendezvous."

Fargo nudged the man away. "No good, son. That's a Ute arrow. The stones that these arrowheads are made from have got a killing power."

Talbot eyed Fargo skeptically. "You wouldn't be pulling a soldier's leg, would you, scout?"

"No, sir. And the name's Fargo. That arrowhead's got to be dug out and right quick." He glanced at the men holding Talbot in a sitting position. "Hold the colonel like he is, boys. Keep him steady." He removed a bullet from Talbot's *cartridge belt. He placed the bullet between Talbot's front teeth. "Bite down, sir. This is going to hurt some."*

*Then he placed one hand to the bloody clothing over the wound, steadying the shoulder area that he knew was about to start flinching uncontrollably. He brought up the Bowie knife, and began carving.*

And then he was standing in the colonel's office here at Fort Survival in the present, years later, that vivid memory triggered by Talbot's offhand remark to Lara. The viewing screen into the past became a window again, looking out upon the busy fort.

Talbot stretched his left arm.

"It still hurts like hell when it rains," he said. "But this being West Texas, that isn't terribly often." His expression grew bleak. His eyes shifted to Fargo. "And now, all of these years later, the scout who saved my life that day walks into my office. It's good to see you, Fargo."

"Good to see you again, Colonel."

"I admit that you have crossed my mind from time to time, scout. I've wondered what became of you." Talbot placed his elbows on his desk, joining his hands at his chin as he studied Fargo. "Right now, I can't help wondering what you're doing here."

Lara rose from her chair.

"Mr. Fargo is in my employ, Colonel. And what you have been discussing is interesting, I assure you. But now, I would like to discuss my brother."

# 8

Fargo remained leaning against the windowsill, observing the confrontation between the steel-backboned, upper-crust young lady from Boston and the crusty military commander. It was, in Fargo's estimation, an even match.

"The first thing I would say regarding your brother," said Colonel Talbot, carefully, "is that in my initial estimation I found him to be a fine soldier. His performance of duties and command of his men was exemplary. He was respected and well liked, although untested in battle."

Lara stood before his desk. "That makes a big difference out here, being in battle I mean."

"As a soldier, of course it does."

"It seems that no one is accepted out here until they have been tested in some way," she said, "either by man or by the elements."

The colonel ran a thumb across his closely cropped white mustache. "Yes, I suppose that is the Western way."

"Well," she said, "if Jeffrey had been tested, you would not hold the opinion you now do."

"And what is that, miss?"

"Why, you filed a report to the War Department in Washington that my brother was a deserter."

"It was the only conclusion I could arrive at," said

Talbot evenly. "To be brutally frank, miss, I would have preferred to have reported that your brother was killed or even missing in action. Deserter is a brand no man can live down in the eyes of others, least of all himself."

"And why wasn't my brother declared missing in action? Washington could not help me with the details, Colonel, which is why I've come to you."

"He could hardly be declared missing in action," said Talbot, "when there was no action. Your brother was riding into what passes for a town out here—a collection of shacks and tents due north, called Shantytown. He was off duty, riding with two fellow officers, for some drinks and poker."

"Was he doing wrong?"

Fargo interjected, "The Army would just as soon its officers spent all of their time in their quarters, polishing their boots and memorizing military rule books. But everyone needs to let off steam. Right, Colonel?"

"That does seem to be the case," said Talbot, "and that's where it gets tricky. Halfway to Shantytown, your brother rode off across the prairie. It was dusk and he soon disappeared from sight. And that is the last anyone has heard or seen of your brother, Miss Newton."

"What did he say to the soldiers, precisely, before he rode off?" Lara asked.

"That is an odd thing." Talbot stroked his mustache with the knuckle of an index finger. "He said nothing. It was, they stated in their reports, as if he were waiting for that point in the trail, at which time he galloped off without a word to them."

"And so your conclusion," she said, "is that he has stayed away of his own volition?"

"He was a good officer," said Talbot. His voice was

steady, but his eyes were sad. "He had good training and discipline."

"And a good upbringing," said Lara, her chin raised.

"Yes, and that," said Talbot. "Miss, please believe me, I implore you. I regret what I had to report about your brother. But the plain truth is that this is a harsh, brutal, demanding duty assignment. Your brother would not be the first young officer trained in the East and sent to the West only to become disillusioned and discouraged, and desert for an easier, better life. The West is a big place, from here to San Francisco and back to Omaha. Your brother could be anywhere."

"Sir," she said sternly, "I regret to say that I find your conclusions wholly unacceptable in light of what I know of Jeffrey."

"And you'll forgive me, ma'am"—steel had returned to Talbot's voice—"but my conclusions are borne out by the evidence and circumstance. Even if your brother encountered hostiles after he left those soldiers, and was slain, he was still a deserter. It pains me to state it so candidly, but you leave me no choice. If your brother was not a deserter, then what is he and where is he?"

"That, sir, is what I have come here to find out. And we will find out what happened to him, won't we, Mr. Fargo?"

Fargo remained at the windowsill.

"I aim to do what I was hired to do."

She crossed the office, to the door. Talbot rose with alacrity and stood to hold open the door for her. She nodded her appreciation.

"When we exchanged telegrams and I informed you that I would be coming out here, Colonel, you were kind enough to offer me accommodations for my stay. I apologize for being plainspoken. I hope that our, uh, words have not caused you to reconsider that kind offer."

He smiled. "Of course not. Another thing about us men of the West, ma'am; we become accustomed to plainspoken women. Yes, civilian quarters are maintained here for visitors, and two separate rooms are presently unoccupied and will, I trust, provide suitable accommodations for you and Fargo. And please avail yourself of my office if I can be of any assistance."

"Colonel, was there a search for my brother?"

"At first. And lawmen in adjacent territories were telegraphed and sent a description. But this fort is undermanned, and my primary mission is to patrol and protect the settlers against hostiles."

"I understand. Thank you, Colonel." She glanced at Fargo. "We'll be leaving now," she said emphatically.

Fargo got the hint, but remained at the windowsill.

"I'll catch up with you," he said. "I'd like to have a few words in private with the colonel."

The flash of anger in her eyes told him that she hadn't expected this. She hesitated in the doorway, studying first him and then the man holding the door for her.

"Men!" she said with an annoyed exhalation of breath.

She stepped outside.

Talbot closed the door and returned to his desk. He leaned back in his chair and chuckled. "A spirited young filly."

"That's her," said Fargo.

"I like her spirit." Talbot reached across his desk, opened a humidor, and extended it to Fargo. "Cigar?"

Fargo nodded and Talbot tossed one to him. The

colonel stuck a cigar in the corner of his mouth, struck a match, and puffed fire to it.

Fargo sniffed his cigar. His eyebrows arched as he struck a match and enjoyed working up a halo of smoke. "Much obliged." Both men sat for a rare moment of silence as they enjoyed a few draws.

"You wouldn't happen to know a fellow name of Sanford, would you, Colonel?"

"Are we talking about the big shot over in El Paso?"

"We are."

Talbot shrugged. "I've met him a few times when the army met with the El Paso Businessman's Association. Sanford was their president. Don't remember much about him, tell you the truth. Everyone in this country knows of him. Heard he was thinking of running for office. Why are you asking about him?"

"Just a thought. Miss Newton knows him. So did her brother."

Talbot paused in his enjoyment of smoking to study his cigar.

"A good cigar is supposed to mean something between men, scout. Are we just a couple of old soldiers playing catch up here, or are you trying to get something out of me?"

"A little of both," said Fargo. "And, sir, I am not a soldier. I'm a civilian. And you've got something up your sleeve besides an old arrowhead wound. I'm curious, Colonel. Why did you tell Miss Newton about what happened that day on the river?"

"I was softening her up."

"Beg your pardon, sir?"

"I remember a few things about you, scout, from those years back, and I don't imagine you've changed much."

"Uh, what exactly are you referring to, sir?"

"I may have gotten older, but I'm not blind yet, scout. You're working for Lara Newton. She's a beautiful young woman. If you haven't gotten under her petticoat by now, I'm sure it's not for lack of trying."

"Actually, sir, it's the other way around." Fargo shook his head, irritated with the conversation. "Regardless, I'm a little confused. What the hell are we talking about? Why are we discussing Lara Newton's petticoats?"

"Because we're two men smoking good cigars and not bullshitting each other," said Talbot, "and mainly because history is about to repeat itself." Talbot rested both elbows on his desk and smoked intently. "You're going to have to put your love life on hold, Fargo, because the Army needs you again. I'm heading out tomorrow, by myself, for a meeting with Chief White Feather. It's a meeting of vital importance toward reining in some of the hostiles that have been terrorizing this region. That's why I told the story about that day on the Piedra. Miss Newton feigned polite interest, but I watched her eyes as I spoke. She took new measure of you as a man. She will now accept you riding out with us tomorrow. You do know this country. I remember you telling me that once in Colorado."

"I know it," said Fargo. "The problem, sir, is that I'm not out here wasting time on romance. This time I'm tied up making money. Miss Newton has hired me. I've signed on with her. I can't run out on her."

"No one's asking you to," said Talbot. "You're postponing your work for her, which you'll resume upon our return. We'll only be gone for two days."

"Only? Colonel, you just met the lady. Did she seem like the patient type to you?"

"That's why I softened her up," said Talbot. "You take care of the rest."

"Why, I'm much obliged for that," said Fargo without enthusiasm. "Nice smoking cigars with you, Colonel, but I don't think so."

Talbot tossed his half-smoked cigar into a spittoon beside his desk. "You were hoping you could wheedle information out of me about that young lady's brother, but the truth of the matter is that I told her everything I know. There's big trouble brewing in these parts, Fargo. I'm not going to lie about that. There are bands of marauders making life a miserable hell for good folks trying to settle this land. Renegade Utes? These are in the same class. I won't even repeat some of the atrocities they've committed."

"Who's their leader?"

"Doesn't seem to be one," said Talbot. "Gangs living off the land, and renegades. They've got to be stopped, and I don't want the Piedra River incident to happen again. White Feather says he knows something and he'll only talk to me, so I'm riding out to meet him."

"I don't know why I'm telling you this," Fargo sighed, "but I know old White Feather. He was always on the side of keeping the peace as long as his people were left with their dignity."

"He still feels that way. But he's a tough old bird. There's a new source of rifles flooding into the wrong hands in this country, and White Feather sent word that he knows something about it."

"Like you say, he's a tough old bird and inscrutable as hell." Fargo tugged an earlobe. "Colonel, there is the possibility that it's a trap."

Talbot nodded. "Or there could be trouble along the way to White Feather's camp. It's a one-day ride, and I'm due to meet with him tomorrow night. Fargo, I didn't expect you to walk into this office, but since fate chose to put you here, I'll level with you. The Army needs you. Those settlers are trying to make a civilization for the future out of this frontier. They are hard-working families. They need you. I've got to meet with White Feather, and you're the scout I need to do it. I can't make that an order, scout, but I damn well wish I could."

Fargo took an extended draw on his cigar, and when he exhaled, twin streams of smoke expelled from his nostrils with a sigh. He tossed the half-finished cigar into the spittoon from across the room.

"Damn, Colonel, you ought to consider running for political office. You're a silver-tongued devil."

"I only speak the truth," said Talbot. "Do you ride with me, or not?"

"All right, all right," said Fargo. "What time?"

"0600 hours. And do me the courtesy, scout, of being punctual this time."

"Yes, sir."

Fargo started out of the office.

Talbot said, "And, Skye . . . thanks."

Fargo's response was to close the door after him on his way out of the Colonel's office.

He found the Ovaro where he'd left it, tethered to the hitching post in front of the headquarters building. He untethered the horse, gave its mane a ruffle, and swung into the saddle.

There was no sign of Lara's dun, which had been tethered alongside the Ovaro when they went in to see the colonel. *Stabled*, Fargo figured.

Having resigned himself to this new turn of events, Fargo next wanted to investigate more of the background while he had the opportunity, before the column moved out in the morning. He rode at a canter halfway to the front gate.

Lara stepped up to intercept him from the shade of a veranda. She held a parasol against the midday sun. "Fargo, where are you going?"

He looked at the structure behind her. "How are the accommodations?"

"Modest. Adequate. A room for you, a room for me. The colonel is being most generous. But where are you going?"

"I've taken on a two-day job with the Army, as scout," said Fargo. "I leave with the colonel at 0600 tomorrow morning."

She drew herself erect. "But that is unthinkable. You are a man of honor. You and I have an agreement. What about finding out what happened to Jeffrey?"

"It's our best shot at getting information. I'll be at the center of the colonel's entire command throughout these next forty-eight hours, and when I get back from having spent that time on the trail with this company of cavalrymen, I'll know something about your brother, at least more than I do now."

She considered this. "Is it true what the colonel said, about you and the Indian?"

"It was something I had to do," said Fargo. "I'd rather not have done it, but a message had to be sent. It got through. A job had to be done. And that's the way it is now."

"You behave as if I don't have any say in the matter."

"This is bigger than a few people," said Fargo. "Tell me again how you remember your brother."

She took a step back, with a blink.

"Haven't I made it clear? Jeffrey was a man of

honor, bravery, and commitment. It is inconceivable that he would desert."

"His first commitment then," said Fargo, "would be to maintaining the peace in this country, and from what I hear, there's only one chance to do that in these parts, and that's what the colonel has asked me to be a part of."

"I see. You're saying that my brother would want you to do this?"

"That's exactly what I'm saying." There she was again, he thought, fast as a whip. "What do you say?" he asked.

"Very well." She shifted her parasol for a better look up at him in the saddle, and had to squint because the sun shone in her eyes. "As long as you and I understand that you will quietly probe for information about Jeffrey while you're on this . . . this expedition. But what about you?" she asked. "Where are you going now?"

"I'm heading out for a ride."

"I can see that. Where are you going?"

"I'm gong to track down some information. And a man's got to have some leisure time."

"But . . . what about me? What am I supposed to do?"

"With all due respect, hon," said Fargo, "let me do my job. For the time being, sit on your pretty backside and like it."

He kneed the Ovaro and cantered off, away from her.

She stood, watching him ride out through the main gate, her fists clenched at her sides. She whispered to his back, for her own ears only.

"I'll do neither, you arrogant son of a bitch."

# 9

Her name was Candy, and she was sweet as could be, red-haired and freckled, with dancing green eyes and the cutest dimples. She couldn't have been more than twenty, and she still had a delightfully jiggly layer of baby fat that made her even prettier in her curve-clinging satin maroon nightgown. Her melon-shaped breasts looked like they wanted to burst out of the tight lacy bodice that confined them, their milky whiteness smooth and creamy above the lace while, just below, the shapes of her erect nipples poked to get through the clinging fabric. The hem of the nightie ended at midthigh.

She sat sideways on Fargo's lap. Fargo was bare-chested, wearing only his britches. His hat was over in the corner with his boots. His shaft was growing hard beneath her plump bottom. She was running her fingers through his hair.

Whores came in every size, shape, color, and description in the West. There were the hard-edged boozers who took laudanum to smother their bleak reality while sweaty cowhands and miners and farmers used their sagging bodies. Then there were the fancy sporting gals—prime specimens of womanhood dolled up in powder and paint and finery. There were the expensive ones, most likely to snag themselves a proposal of marriage from a widowed landowner or an honest man of steady means who could take them out of this trade or possibly even a rancher or mining magnate who sought merely to install a personal, always-available love slave in a cabin "outside of town." There were women who had come to the West and found themselves widowed, their children dead of the diseases that accounted for a seventy percent infant mortality rate below the age of five. Such women often drifted downward into prostitution.

And there were girls like Candy—girls whose parents were deceased, or who perhaps had shamed their family or run off to conquer the world and were now too ashamed of what they'd done to return home— having joined the sisterhood of the world's oldest profession, which thrived out here where, in most communities, the only women were wives, widows, and whores. The profession thrived in a land populated by wandering, worldly men without women. Young women like Candy would have six months to a year before they lost the radiant freshness that allowed madams, like the old crone who ran this place, to fetch top dollar for them.

Candy was almost jolly, fresh off the farm, not too much education, not too bright, but Fargo sensed a kindness in her heart that made him like her. He kept thinking of what the seasoned old madam had called to him as he'd walked up the stairs, as she recounted the money he'd paid her.

"Now you try to be careful with this one, dearie. She's brand-new. You're her first. You're breaking her in, cowboy. So don't let me catch you slapping her around if she don't do what you tell her fast enough. You hear me? You call me if she acts up."

"Shut up," Fargo had told the old crone.

So here he was with this delicious little morsel sitting in his lap, as he rested one hand on her hip to steady her where she sat. His other hand seemed to have a mind of its own, and drifted up to palm the roundness of her left breast. The erect nipple burned against his palm. She moaned softly. She wore a subtle perfume that somehow made her farm girl aura even more arousing to him.

He'd trotted the Ovaro into Shantytown thirty minutes earlier and found the motley collection of clapboard shacks and pitched tents along a single deeply rutted, clogged street, everything he expected. He'd been in—or passed through or, more often, ridden around—hundreds of these overnight boom towns that sprang up near military outposts on the frontier. The air was filled with the tinkling sounds of honky-tonk pianos, punctuated occasionally by raised shouts of arguing men, and more than once, by a roar of gunfire that settled the dispute.

A shot of rotgut whisky with a warm beer chaser, and he tipped the barman more than he should have for directions to the best place for action in town.

He had passed inspection by the madam, an over-rouged, bony, befeathered gal who took his money, clinically administered the washbowl-warm water and soap treatment of his privates, and directed him up the flight of stairs to the door of this bedroom.

A bed next to an open window was the only piece of furniture in the room other than the chair upon which Fargo sat with the girl.

"So what would you like, mister?" A certain innocent enthusiasm rippled through the breathy words she whispered into his ear. "You've paid for it. It's your pleasure. They, uh, they taught me how to do some different kinds of things I never knew about and"—the kid actually blushed and lowered her eyes—"and of course I just plain like to, you know, do it."

He had befriended his share of fallen doves over the years, and faulted no woman or man for playing the hand fate dealt them as long as it did not involve them harming others. Fate was often cruel.

He exerted extreme self-control, mentally commanding his hand to lower. His hand left her plump breasts and rested on her thigh. This did nothing to quell his throbbing member, which she surely felt pulsating against her bottom. He was not sure he wanted to be the man to initiate this sweet girl into whoredom.

And there was the real reason why he was here. He was here for information, not sex. A whorehouse was the best place in the world for learning secrets and digging up dirt.

"Reckon I've got a surprise for you," he said.

There was a catch in her breath. She was intrigued.

"Is that so?"

"I just want you to tell me about yourself."

She giggled a cute giggle, covering her mouth. She blushed again.

"They told me that there'd be men like you, who'd pay me to talk before they . . . you know. But I didn't think it would happen with my very first, uh, customer!" She sat up straight in his lap, took a deep breath that seemed to expand her boobs in their lacy confinement, and asked, sweetly enough, but as if reciting from a memorized script, "Would you like to hear what a young girl like me does with herself when she's alone? Or would you like to hear about what I saw two of the other girls doing last night?"

Despite an intense curiosity, Fargo relented to the task at hand.

"No, I mean really," he said, trying to maintain a level speaking voice. "You're a sweet kid, but Candy isn't your real name, is it?"

"Of course not, silly."

"Well, that's what I want to know, for starters."

She studied him, her head tilted slightly. "You're a strange one, mister."

"Not really. What's your name, Candy?"

"Jenny," she said in a small voice. "I was separated from my folks in Fort Worth. We was heading west. I've been looking for them town to town, but last week my money ran out. I did chores for a few days but, well, a girl's got to eat steady." She drew another deep breath and faced him with an optimistic smile. "And, well, here I am, mister, doing the best I can to stay alive. Why do you want to know stuff like that?"

"I wanted to see if I was right about you. I was."

"What do you mean?"

"You're a good girl, aren't you, Jenny?"

Her eyes dropped. Some of her bravado disappeared. "I was."

"I believe you'll tell me the truth if I ask you a question, and I've tried to establish with you that I'm serious. This doesn't have anything to do with the games they taught you here."

She brought her eyes back to his and her fingers drifted again through strands of his untrimmed hair. "Yes, sir," she said like a good little whore. "Only I've got to say, honey, you're one feller I wouldn't mind playing games with and I do mean for free. You're big and strong and handsome, and the only time you talk is when you've got something to say. Are you a cowboy?"

"I've worked as a cowboy."

"See? You ain't the only one knows how to read sign in a person. Are you an outlaw?"

"I don't ride the desperado trail."

She became contrite. "I didn't mean to get personal."

He chuckled. "I thought that's what old boys like me and gals like you did, Jenny. Get personal that is."

Her fingertips went to stroking the hairs at the back of his head, dancing across his skin. Her rump felt fine as ever, seated there on Fargo's lap. His pulsing staff had only increased in size.

"Jenny," she said. "I like the way you say my real name."

"Call me Skye, honey."

"Okay, Skye honey."

*Hoo boy,* thought Fargo.

He whispered into her ear. "Speaking of desperados, I am trying to get some information for a friend."

She purred at the sensation of his breath in her ear, and rotated her rump. A shiver coursed through her, making the milky-white globes of her breasts quiver.

"Ooh, that feels good when you whisper in my ear, Skye honey."

"Have you been in this house long enough to hear the other girls talk?" he asked in the same whisper. "Have you heard them say anything about the marauders that are working around here?"

"Well, sure. You know how girls are."

"Don't reckon as I do. Anyway, what have you heard?"

She shrugged. Fargo was concentrating on her every word, but could not take his eyes off the way her breasts jiggled with her every movement under her maroon satin nightie. The shrug had made her nipples seem to stare straight up at him from their lacy confinement.

"Well, I've heard that there are gangs raising hell with the settlers and the miners," she said. "Doesn't everyone know that?"

"What else have you heard?"

Another shrug. "This morning, when we were closed and Miss Sara wasn't around—that's the madam."

"We've met," said Fargo. "What did you hear?"

"A couple of the girls had taken care of some mighty rough fellows. Turns out the roughnecks didn't know each other, but each was here and this morning they was talking about it."

"And what were the girls talking about, sweetie?" asked Fargo, patiently as he could.

She pressed herself to him and breathed warmly into his ear, her tongue darting. "Skye honey, I'd love to lick you all over. I'll make you a deal."

He kept trying like the devil to remind himself that this was supposed to be work, that he was here to get the lay of the land, so to speak. "Um, uh, what kind of deal?"

At least, he told himself, he hadn't removed his hands from around her waist. Business, he kept telling himself. He was here for information.

She drew back a few inches so that her green eyes stared straight into his gaze. Hers was smoky, her cheeks were flushed, and her breathing came shallow. He felt enveloped in the musky scent of her.

"Here's what I'd like to see happen," she said. "You're here to try to get me to give you some information. And maybe I've got some information to pass along that you could use. But see, I've got something that I want from you."

This perplexed him. "Is that right?"

"That's right," she said. "See, I figure from here on out, the fellers that walk up them stairs to do things to me are going to be doing just that—I mean, *doing* things *to* me, you understand? I'd sort of like my first, uh, time here to be . . . doing those things with a nice feller, not some smelly bugger I wouldn't look at on the street. What I'm saying, Skye honey, is that you most likely are the last gentle man that will ever touch me that way, you know? And that's what I want you to do. If I've got to do this to stay alive in this here house, I want my first time to be the best. Okay?"

"Almost sounds reasonable, the way you put it," said Fargo. "Dang, but you women are the most unpredictable critters. First, tell me what it is you think I want to know."

"Well, I did hear Gladys and Jasmine—well, Jasmine's not her real name—but anyway, they both heard their customers bragging to them that outfits they ride for ain't riding with each other, don't even know each other, but there is one big shot somewhere, some white man, who's keeping it going and running things."

This was almost enough for Fargo's manhood to stop palpitating.

Almost.

"How is this person keeping it going?"

Another of her delectable shrugs. "By selling guns cheap to the gangs, taking a cut of the profits, telling them where the Army patrols are going to be so they know where not to strike, that sort of thing. I gathered that's all these outlaw fellers told the girls, who was mostly talking about what mean bastards they was. So is that good enough for my part of the bargain, Skye honey?"

"Reckon it is. Do you want me to call you Candy or Jenny?"

She indicated their surroundings. "In this place, I'm Candy. And now I'm going to collect on *my* part of our deal."

She slid off his lap like a curvaceous snake, and before he knew it, she was on her knees before him, tugging off his britches. When the buckskins cleared his midsection, his hardened member sprang up like a soldier snapping to attention.

Candy made a contented sound deep in her throat, purring at the sight. She discarded the britches with a careless toss over her shoulder in the general direction of his other clothing. She moved forward, to between his legs, and caressed his hardness with a loving cupping of her hands. She lowered her mouth to deliver butterfly kisses with the darting of a wet, hot tongue here and there, before she lowered her mouth over it.

Fargo ran his fingers through her red hair. He stretched his legs out straight before him. He rested his head against the back of his chair as she began bobbing her head.

Fractions of a second short of exploding, he gently guided her head away from him.

She looked up with confusion and concern.

"What . . . ?" she started to say.

In one smooth motion, he stood and scooped her up in both of his arms.

"I like to give as well as receive," he told her.

He flung her on the bed. She landed with a happy squeal. Fargo leaped down onto her and they tussled and cooed and felt each other for a while before she ended up on top.

Her hair was tangled into red ringlets. Beads of perspiration like pearls along her upper lip. Her lips were swollen from kissing. Fargo hadn't gotten around to taking off her nightie, which was plastered to her every delicious curve. Straddling him, she reached down. Her fingers encircled his erection, guiding it.

"Be gentle," she whispered in his ear.

She lowered her mouth to his for another torrid kiss as she positioned her body onto the length of his shaft.

He let her set the pace, which was easy and rocking at first, a lot of kissing and groping. But before long, the easy rocking became hungry with need, and so did her breathing. Fargo exercised self-control and held back on his climax as her pelvis twisted this way and that with his erection buried deep inside her.

Then she was shuddering, bucking atop him like she was having a seizure as a wave of pleasure swept through her. It was more than a minute before her shuddering began to subside.

"Oh, g-goodness . . ." she cooed into his ear, her face on the pillow beside him. "Skye honey, I've never had it that good in my whole durn life!"

"Then let's have some more," said Fargo.

He retained his hardness, and so was able to rotate her around so that she was beneath him—with Fargo assuming the dominant position—without his uncoupling from her or loosening his hold on the globes of her sweet bubble-butt. Then he started slamming her hard and fast. Her cooing and mewing turned to primal grunting that matched his own. Her fingers clawed and pounded at his back. He lowered his head, without slackening his pumping pace, and began sucking first one of her nipples through the sweat-clinging satin, then the other.

"Oh, Skye honey!"

Another series of quaking climaxes shuddered

through her and this time he let himself go, exploding within her steamy tightness so that they soared and their lives became timeless together. Then they collapsed into a sweaty, heavily breathing, entwined, contentedly murmuring heap, and some time later she drifted off to sleep in his arms.

In the heat of the afternoon, she woke briefly, crying.

He kissed the tangled red mop of her hair.

"What is it, honey?"

"I was just thinking." She sniffed. "Working here . . . Skye honey, well damn. That's the last good time I'll ever have!"

He stroked her hair and told her that things would be all right, and she drifted off to sleep again.

When she next awakened, late-afternoon sunshine was shafting in through the bedroom's one window. Fargo had slid out of bed a few minutes earlier, leaving her head resting on the pillow as she slept on her side. When she opened her eyes, she was staring straight at the stack of money he'd placed on the bedside table. She blinked once, twice, and the green eyes came awake.

She twisted around and saw Fargo, who had just finished dressing, strapping on his gunbelt, with the holstered Colt around his waist.

Her eyes widened. She sat up. The sheets dropped away to reveal her melon-shaped, milky-white breasts topped with oversized, pink aureoles. Becoming fully awake, she realized her nakedness and covered her nudity with reflexive, maidenly modesty, drawing the sheet up to her neck.

"Skye honey, where are you going?"

He turned to face her from the foot of the bed. She looked tousled, uncertain, and vulnerable.

"It's time for us to say good-bye."

"Will . . . will we see each other again?"

"I doubt it," he said, "but stranger things have happened in this country. Anyway, I want to thank you, Jenny. You're fine people."

"Skye, you're the most incredible man I've ever—" She didn't seemed to know how to finish. She nodded at the stack of money. "What's this for? Miss Sara explained to me that she gets paid before a gentleman comes up here, and I get my share once a month after room and board."

The fact of the matter was that the stack of money on the bedside table was most of what Lara Newton had paid him up front during a brief rest in their ride from El Paso the night before. She had promised to have the rest wired in. Thinking of Lara, he felt a jolt of guilt that caught him by surprise. Then he took another look at the lush form of the redhead, every inch of her discernible through damp sheets clinging to her lush body. . . .

"Is there a stage through this rat-hole of a town?" he asked.

"Yes. That's how I ended up here. Shantytown was as far as my money would take me."

He cocked his hat just right, and nodded to indicate the money.

"Take that and buy yourself a new beginning somewhere down the line. This isn't a life for you, Jenny. Tell me the word and I'll make sure that Miss Sara, and whatever strong-arm friends she's got, let you walk out of here and don't come after you." He leaned over and delivered a chaste kiss to the top of her tangled carrot-top head. That musky love scent clung to her, caressing his nostrils, enticing him. But he pulled back. He crossed the bedroom and hesitated with his hand on the door handle. "Give me the word, Jenny. Do you want that new beginning?"

"Skye honey, I'd forgotten how beautiful . . . it can be. Like a sacred thing, almost. Oh yes, I do want to escape from here! And I wish it could be with you . . ."

"Now that's wishing for a mite too much," said Fargo. "You take that money, honey. Move on. You'll do all right if you make good choices. A nice family will take you in to help raise their young ones. Or you'll reunite with your folks. What time is that stage due?"

"In about an hour."

"I want to see you on it."

Then he left without another glance at her. Closing the door behind him, he went clumping down the stairs, passing a gent who was on his way up to one of the other rooms.

The madam met Fargo, at the bottom of the stairs, with a leer. With her bony features, feathers, and rouge she reminded him of a blushing skeleton.

"Well, honey, was that new tart of ours sweet enough for you?"

Fargo reached for his wallet, and plunked the remainder of his down payment onto the woman's hand.

She stared down at the sizable wad of money. "Sweet crimeny, what's this for?"

"That's to buy Candy's way out of here."

She looked up at him with calculating eyes. "Look here, mister, I work for tough boys—you understand me?" She nodded to the room at the top of the stairs. "That there piece of tail is an investment."

"I'm tough enough to leave them bleeding," Fargo said in a quiet voice. "That girl's going to be on the next stage out. You can tell your tough bosses that if anyone tries to stop her, they're dead. Or as far as you know"—he nodded to the money—"that's just between you and me, and she slipped out before you knew it, you were so busy running such a fine whorehouse. Now that must happen once in a while."

"It does."

"So how does that sound, Miss Sara?"

She continued staring at the cash, then looked up back at him. "Reckon it sounds reasonable enough."

"Good. Because if there're any complications, if that young lady is detained or harmed in any way, I'll come back here and burn this place to the ground. Just so you know." He tipped his hat. "Good day to you, Miss Sara."

She was already wadding the money down the front of her peacock-feathered cleavage. "Good day to you, mister. And good riddance."

He crossed the street, and entered the same honky-tonk he'd been in earlier. He ordered another mug of warm beer from the same bartender, and sat at a table by a fly-specked window. He felt that sense of complete wellness one feels after an afternoon of lovemaking. He nursed the beer and before long Jenny emerge from the ramshackle, two-story structure that was Miss Sara's whorehouse.

She stood waiting, holding a small traveling case. She kept looking around, as if expecting to see Fargo.

Fargo remained where he was and finished his beer with a slurp as he watched the stagecoach carry her out of Shantytown.

He left the honky-tonk, mounted the patient Ovaro and—flat-ass broke—rode back toward Fort Survival as night descended.

# 10

The following morning, Fargo stood on the veranda of the headquarters building, enjoying his favorite time of the day, that first silvery freshness preceding the dawn.

The fort was stirring to life. Windows of the barracks were alight, and the latrines were getting a lot of traffic. Men were grumbling awake. Horses were beginning to whinny, and there was already activity in the stable area. Morning formation was fast approaching. The smell of bacon and sausage from the mess hall wafted across the parade ground.

The Ovaro was tethered to the hitching rail in front of Headquarters, as was Colonel Talbot's horse, a chestnut mare.

There was as yet no sign of Colonel Talbot. Fargo had made a point of being early for their appointment. He'd just had a breakfast of eggs, sausage, toast, and a few gallons of coffee, sharing a table with the company cookie, who had his lackeys gearing up for the morning rush. He and Fargo shot the breeze about the beauty of the Bitterroot Valley up Montana way, and how fine the fishing would be this time of year. Cookie was a nice fella, and Fargo had found that it paid to be on friendly terms with the cook whether you were on the trail, with the garrison, or anywhere else.

The first rays of morning sunlight touched him, and felt good. The fact that he was early for his meet with the colonel, plus his pleasures of yesterday followed by a good night's sleep—and a fine breakfast— had him feeling better than he figured any man had a right to feel.

A feminine clearing of the throat, and footsteps upon the boardwalk, brought his attention around. Lara Newton was approaching. Her blond hair was tied back with a blue bow that matched her dress. Her blue eyes were serious, and so was the line of her mouth.

And all of a sudden, he wasn't feeling quite so great. He experienced the stirring of apprehension combined with a pang of guilt.

When he'd returned to the fort last night from Shantytown, after sunset, he had seen light behind the drawn curtain of Lara's window, the guestroom next to his. He'd put up the Ovaro at the company stable, in a "guest" stall next to Lara's dun, then tried to be as quiet as possible when returning to the guest billet and letting himself into his room. But she would not be able to help but hear the fall of his boot heels and the clink of his spurs. It had been too early for sleep yet she had made no attempt to knock on his door and communicate with him. He had left well enough alone.

He'd lain awake, his arms curved behind his head, staring up at the ceiling. He would have preferred looking at the stars, but looking at the ceiling was just as good for thinking about the information that had filtered to him this day. He fell asleep reviewing that information. . . .

There was no sign of Lara that morning when he rose, refreshed, and went to make friends with Cookie in the mess. He'd been wondering when he would see Lara again.

"Well, there you are." There was an icy snip to her words.

"And there you are," he responded as amiably as he could. "Good morning, Lara. Beautiful day."

"Where did you go yesterday, after you left here?"

He gazed off to the east, to buy a few moments to think. A little foreplay back at Sanford's mansion—for her pleasure alone—and here she was, behaving like a shrewish wife confronting an errant husband. On the other hand, he *was* working for her, and considering the sad state of his finances—lower than snake shit, as they said back in East Texas—it would be prudent to be humble.

"I was in Shantytown, getting information for us."

"For us, eh?" She looked him up and down. "Right. I heard some of the soldiers speaking of Shantytown last night. I understood that it was no town at all, but a ratty collection of gambling dens and houses of ill repute."

"Ill?" said Fargo. "Those joints were alive and kicking last night."

"That, I think, is more than I need to know. And what sort of information did you obtain for *us*?" She emphasized the last word with sarcasm.

"We haven't got time right now for me to tell you that, and the truth is, I haven't made sense out of it myself." He'd fallen asleep last night with unanswered questions plaguing him. "Uh, the point is, Lara, this information, uh, cost me some money."

She arched an eyebrow, and folded her arms before her. "And why, pray, are you telling me this if you don't intend to tell me what you've been doing and what you've learned?"

He nodded. "Hmm, good point." He found himself scratching the back of his neck, squinting into the first rays of the rising sun. "As a matter of fact, my visit to Shantytown cost me every dang dollar I had."

She regarded him coolly. "Gambling or a girl?"

"I told you. Information. I don't know what to do with it yet, but it cost me. The sad fact of the matter is, Lara, I'm stone broke."

"Sad for you, perhaps," she said. "I, on the other hand, tend to be financially astute in matters of commerce."

"I'll bet you do," Fargo muttered, seeing where this was heading. "That's your Boston upper-crust way of telling me you're not about to advance me any more of my retainer."

Her lips quirked, the trace of a smile. "I knew you weren't as obtuse as you pretended to be."

"'Obtuse.' Another word for me to look up. Working for you has broadened my vocabulary—I'll say that much. All right," he said. "Tell me this then, and tell me quick. Was your brother a by-the-book, step-by-step kind of man, or was he independent and inquisitive?"

"The latter, certainly. Even as a child, Jeffrey was curious about everything. He had an eye for detail." She studied Fargo with narrowed eyes. "Why are you asking me this? Please tell me what you know."

The headquarters door opened.

"Later," said Fargo.

Colonel Talbot briskly stepped onto the veranda, with the vigor and demeanor of a man half his age. He wore his riding blues, a tan Stetson, and polished boots. He tipped his hat to Lara. "Miss Newton. You're looking as lovely as the sunrise."

She curtsied slightly, as was customary, with a

smile. "And you, Colonel, are most gallant. I came by to wish you both Godspeed and a safe return."

"Most kind of you," said Talbot. "We'll be back by mid- or late afternoon tomorrow." He turned to Fargo. "Thanks again for agreeing to ride with me, scout, and for your promptness."

"Name's Fargo, sir," Fargo chided, "and if I had to wait much longer, I was going to figure you'd got yourself a case of cold feet."

Talbot ran the tip of his thumb across his close-cropped white mustache, half hiding a grin. "I might, if I had any sense. There could be trouble on this ride. But White Feather extended his invite and I'm obliged to accept it. And we'd best get started if we are to reach his camp by sunset." He started toward his chestnut horse.

Lara said, "Colonel, might I request a favor?"

He paused to face her with an indulgent smile. "My dear, much as I would love to allow you to accompany us, I must insist that you remain behind, here at the fort, until we return."

"I understand that, Colonel." She spoke earnestly. "Believe me, I don't like it, but I understand it. No, my request is that I be allowed to examine my brother's effects, if they've been kept intact."

Talbot nodded without considering the matter.

"Speak with the quartermaster. I had your brother's effects stored in the event that there was an investigation, since his fate is undetermined. The quartermaster will show you where his things are stored, and allow you access to them. Inform him that you have my personal authorization."

"I will. Thank you, sir."

Then Fargo and Talbot rode out through the open front gates.

Fargo gave a farewell wave to Lara, which she returned unenthusiastically.

They rode hard as the day grew warm, traversing rugged land toward a haze-shrouded mountain range across a considerable distance of rolling prairie, emerald-green with scrub brush.

The colonel knew the way, and so Fargo concentrated on their surroundings as they rode; his every sense attuned for any suggestion of a shift in their surroundings that would betray a hostile human presence. He could determine no such presence as they rode on. As far as Fargo could tell, these west Texas badlands belonged to him and the colonel. They worked up a considerable sweat.

At midday, they gave the horses and themselves a rest in the shade provided by a cut in the terrain. While the horses munched from their feedbags of grain, Fargo and Talbot sat in the shade and sipped from their canteens.

"When I last spoke with old White Feather," said Fargo, "it was back when the treaties were first signed. The tribal lands were clearly designated."

Talbot made an unpleasant sound. "It's just like up in the Colorado Territory, and too damn many other places. The politicians let the homesteaders and miners ignore the boundaries declared by the treaties. Before you know it, the tribal councils are spitting war talk, as they've got a right to, and who's called in to keep the peace but the U.S. Cavalry."

Fargo recapped his canteen. "Just one of the reasons I don't much cotton to wearing a uniform, sir. But what about White Feather? When I knew him he was crusty and could be mean as a bear, but he had the heart of an eagle."

Talbot studied him. "You really understand these people, don't you?"

Fargo shrugged. "So do you, sir, or White Feather wouldn't have sent word for a personal meet with you."

"You're right, of course." Talbot sighed. "It's not too difficult to read them if you think fair."

"Sir, is White Feather tied in with these marauders that are raising such hell?"

"I've considered that." Talbot stroked his mustache with the knuckle of an index finger. "I'd prefer to think that the old fox is what he seems to be; a tribal elder on the side of keeping the peace. He understands that for his people to do otherwise is for them to invite defeat and ultimate annihilation. The others of the council listen to him, but they're the ones who distrust the government, the army, and me in particular as I am the personal embodiment to them of our government. That is why they've only agreed to meet if I agreed to come alone or with one scout, with no column of soldiers in sight."

"You're a mighty brave man, Colonel, fixing to ride out here alone. Or am I replacing somebody?"

"No, I was going to ride alone until fate waltzed you into my office yesterday," said Talbot. "I know this country better than most, but you're the best scout I ever did have. With the two of us making this ride, we just might stand half a chance of making it home."

"Thanks for not mentioning that to Miss Newton."

"And why should I? She's a fine young lady, and her coming all this distance to investigate her brother's disappearance indicates good moral fiber. But yes, the risk is considerable, as you must know. This country is crawling with mankillers spoiling for a fight. That's why this meet with White Feather is so damn vital. A talk with the old boy will clear the air and take us closer to putting an end to this lawlessness."

"That," said Fargo, "is mighty idealistic coming from a military man, sir, if you don't mind my saying so. I'd put the reality of a peaceful West at, oh, somewhere around a hundred years from now—if ever."

They continued on. The ground began to climb gradually as they drew nearer to the mountains. They found a trail leading through mesquite and scrub oak.

A mile farther, and they came upon a wagon.

The wagon was on its side. One of its wheels was busted. Its team had been stolen, or else had fled. A man's body lay, facedown, to one side of the trail. A woman's body, at the opposite side of the road, clutched a small bundle of blankets.

Talbot rode over to where the woman lay. He dismounted before Fargo could speak, and knelt down to feel for a pulse, then examined the contents of the bundle.

"My God, it's a child. They're both dead."

The Ovaro whinnied nervously, picking up a scent it did not like.

Fargo patted the horse. "I know," he told the animal. He rested his hand on the butt of his holstered Colt. "Colonel, we'd best be careful. This could be a trap."

"Too late," laughed a sneering voice.

Fargo and Talbot both whirled in the direction of the overturned wagon.

A man had been crouched within the wreckage of the wagon. He now stood, balancing himself, and aiming his rifle at them. He wore a black slouch hat and a black duster.

Talbot stood in place as the man's aim moved from him to Fargo.

"Looks like you were right again, scout," he growled to the man astride the Ovaro.

The man in the wagon spat. "Quit palavering among yourselves, and let me see that iron drop. Go on, drop your guns. I've got to signal the boss. Walking Razor, he's going to let us have some fun with you."

The sneer never left his face as he raised the rifle and triggered off a shot, then levered another round into the chamber and started to bring the rifle back down on Talbot and Fargo. He never completed the motion. Fargo's Colt jumped into his hand and roared once, the gunfire was doubly loud because it was matched by Talbot, who had fast-drawn his revolver and simultaneously triggered a shot. The rifleman was still sneering when the two chunks of flying lead ripped through his heart and splattered from gory exit wounds in his back.

Talbot swung into his saddle.

"I'd say we best make tracks, scout."

Fargo holstered the Colt, scanning their surroundings. "To quote that deceased fella in the wagon, sir . . . too late."

Talbot followed his gaze, and drew up his mount. "Damn. We're snookered."

"That's one word for it," said Fargo.

A dozen riders came galloping in at them from every direction. The riders had concealed themselves in gullies and washes, far enough away from the wagon for neither the Ovaro nor Fargo to sense their presence, yet close enough to respond when the one left behind summoned them with a rifle shot. They thundered in amid a swirling haze of dust, to form a circle around Talbot and Fargo. Steely eyes locked, and knuckles whitened around triggers as the dozen men, clad in black slouch hats and matching dusters, wordlessly stared down their guns, aiming at Fargo and Talbot.

Through the settling dust, a rider dressed in black reined up a coal-black stallion. He wore an eye patch and a calvary officer's hat worn with the brim forward and up. He also wore a week-old stubble of beard. He laughed, revealing rotting teeth.

"Well, well, look what we got here."

Fargo kept his hand on the butt of his holstered Colt. "Question is," he responded quietly, "what have *we* got?"

"Mister, they call me Walking Razor," the man in black sneered. "I even touch you, I draw blood."

Talbot glared at him unflinchingly.

"Sounds like an Indian name."

Walking Razor spat. "The tribe give it to me when they thought I was their brother. That's before I wiped them out and took their women. Ain't that a laugh? Some red devil thinking I'm his brother."

"That was a mistake," Fargo conceded. He nodded at the wreckage of the wagon in the road, and at the bodies. "Get much?"

Another ugly sneer and Walking Razor spat again. "Enough to buy whiskey and whores."

Talbot said, "I'd heard there were white marauders in these parts, much as there are renegades from the tribes."

"Well you got that plumb right, soldier boy," snickered Walking Razor, "and I'm Exhibit A. But you and this dumb-ass scout are dead wrong to pick this time riding up. Looks like we ain't about to get much from you."

One of the men muttered, "Them boots the soldier boy is wearing would fit me right nice."

Walking Razor sighed. He drew his pistol, aimed it at the man who had spoken, and fired.

The round caught the man between the eyes, pitching him from the saddle.

Walking Razor holstered his pistol. He snarled irritably. "Goddamnit, how many times do I got to say it? First pickings go to me. Always. That goes for women . . . and it goes for boots." His one eye watched the horsemen, who kept their rifles and their attention on Fargo and Talbot, as if one of their own had not just been slaughtered in front of them. "Is there anyone else here who don't understand what I just said?" Walking Razor demanded.

There was no response from the riders.

Talbot said to Fargo, "Damn, and I thought I was a hard-ass."

"Go on, soldier boy," growled the one-eyed man. "Crack wise while you've got the chance, cause you ain't got long left. Now you boys drop them irons and get down off those horses, or my boys will blow you to kingdom come where you sit."

Fargo dropped his Colt to the ground.

Talbot seemed to be watching him to cue him on what to do, and so the colonel likewise dropped his pistol.

Fargo said, "Just out of curiosity, Walking Razor, who the hell are you boys working for?"

The single eye glittered like a dagger point. "And what makes you think I'm working for anybody?"

"Word gets around."

"Yeah. I bet you was talking to them whore bitches at Madam Sara's in Shantytown. I'm going to have to have me a word with that old gash so's she keeps them whores from gossiping. Or I'll do me some cutting my own self. But right now let's talk about you two unlucky sons of bitches. I told you to dismount. Do it."

Fargo did so.

As Talbot dismounted, he saw Fargo slip the knife from his boot up the sleeve of his buckskin shirt.

Their eyes met, silently acknowledging what had happened.

Walking Razor snarled, "Grab their useless hides, you worthless sons."

Half of his riders slid their rifles into scabbards and dismounted, rushing forward, while the others kept their rifles trained on the prisoners. Ruffians manhandled Fargo and Talbot from every side.

"Get a fire built," said Walking Razor. "I got a hankering to burn these boys to death. Let's roast them, real slow."

# 11

The hot noonday sun blazed down without remorse.

Fargo and Talbot had been thrown to the ground, forced to sit back to back, and bound together with a heavy hemp rope binding their arms to their sides. Their legs were free, but this did them little good, awkwardly positioned as they were.

Walking Razor's men had spent the preceding fifteen minutes gathering up twigs and branches, and were just now placing dry leaves for kindling.

Much whiskey was being imbibed. Blood madness was in the air, and the bottles of rotgut being passed around fueled the savagery. An argument broke out between two of the men concerning the fellatio capabilities of a whore in Waco, and one of the men shot the other five times over the issue.

Walking Razor stood apart. Insanity gleamed from his single eye, but of a cold, dangerous sort not confused by kill lust. He raised his revolver and fired. That got everyone's attention.

"Knock off the horseplay! Get that fire started!"

After he and Talbot had been kicked at for a while, and then temporarily ignored, Fargo shifted his arm slightly, and the hidden knife slid into his hand. While Walking Razor oversaw his men gathering firewood, Fargo began to slice away at the heavily corded hemp that bound him to Talbot. The thickness of the rope, and the necessity of having to saw the blade back and forth in a limited manner so as not to arouse suspicion, made for slow going.

Talbot muttered over his shoulder, "How's it going, scout?"

"Name's Fargo," said Fargo. "Give me another minute. Ready to move, sir?"

"Move than ready."

Their guns had been tossed onto the ground, about ten feet away.

Walking Razor swung his one eye back to Talbot and Fargo. He was the only one not guzzling whiskey.

"Hope you fellers don't mind me letting my boys have them some fun. They ain't burned a man to death slow since them trail herders south of Abilene."

Fargo kept his shoulders steady, continuing to saw at the rope, his and Talbot's bodies shielding the discreet movement from the man with the eye patch.

Nearby, drunks were hooting and hollering as the fire was started. Flames began to crackle. Someone threw a bottle at a rock, and missed. There were curses and drunken laughter. Revolvers were fired in the air.

Fargo said, "Say, Walking Razor. Your fellers seem to have quite a hoot killing off each other. Why take after no-account outsiders like me and this soldier?"

Walking Razor grinned. Black teeth glistened. "I likes to kill people."

Talbot twisted slightly to more effectively shield what Fargo was up to, allowing him to see the outlaw. "I'd have thought you'd have had enough fun for one day, slaughtering that innocent, defenseless family up there on the road."

"I reckon it's like they say," said Walking Razor. "You can't never get enough of a good thing. Now let's us old boys get down to some straight talk before you meet your Maker. What do you say, fellers? What brings you poor mothers' sons out riding in these parts anyway?"

"You mean," said Talbot caustically, "if we tell you, your boys won't throw us onto that fire?"

Walking Razor rested his palms on the grips of the pistols he had holstered at both hips. "Don't mean nothing of the sort." He rocked back and forth, as if enjoying the hellish heat, looking like the devil himself.

"Then why don't you tell us?" said Fargo. "The word all over the territory is that that the raiders, outlaws like you boys, and the renegades from the tribes, have been taking orders from one man."

Walking Razor slapped his chest with an open palm, making a loud slap like a gunshot.

"Walking Razor don't take orders from nobody. A rider comes to the camp once a month. Different rider every time. He comes with information I can use, like where the pickings are good and where the soldier boys are going to be on patrol, and every couple of months there's a load of rifles they sell—cheap. Good rifles, like the Army got. And yeah, the rider lights out with a cut of what I done made the month before. You call that working for somebody? I call it a good business arrangement. Look here now. Look's like the fire's ready." He called to his men, "Come here and fetch these here boys. Let's have us a fry!"

Fargo's knife blade severed the remaining fibers of the heavily twined hemp, and, in the same motion, he flung the knife at Walking Razor.

The outlaw caught the blade in his throat, straight through his Adam's apple, the knife handle quivering to the hilt. Walking Razor stumbled backward several paces, raising both hands to his throat, his eye and his mouth forming identical O's of total surprise. Then blood gurgled from his mouth. He dropped to his knees.

Fargo and Talbot burst free of their bonds and, without a word to each other, flung themselves at their guns. Each man grabbed a pistol.

Beyond where Walking Razor knelt burbling blood from his mouth and nose while he tried weakly to loosen the knife handle protruding from his throat, the fire began crackling with vigorous orange flame. The men reacted with inebriated slowness, dropping their bottles and reaching for their guns. Fargo and Talbot were already assuming prone firing positions, each triggering off six rapid-fire rounds, and the dozen drunks before them fell like a field of wheat beneath a scythe.

Walking Razor made it to both feet, oblivious to everything but his panic, knowing he was dying, fixated on the knife buried in his throat.

Talbot leaned over and picked up Fargo's Henry. He lever actioned a round into the chamber, and fired.

The bullet struck Walking Razor in his one good eye and blew out the back of his head, pitching his body backward onto the crackling fire where it quickly ignited. The air became ominously dark with smoke and a horrible stench filled the air as Walking Razor's body burned.

Talbot lowered the rifle. He and Fargo stood. He extended the Henry to Fargo.

"Mercy round," he said.

Fargo holstered his Colt and took the rifle. He had no comment. He retrieved the toothpick from Walking Razor's flaming body and turned to stalk off toward the Ovaro trotting over to meet him, man and beast each taking care to sidestep the sprawled bodies.

Fargo swung astride the Ovaro. "Things seem to have gotten kind of quiet around here, Colonel. I suggest that we move with all due haste."

The colonel's chestnut approached. Talbot swung into the saddle.

"Suggestion approved. Good work, Fargo. You're right. Let's make tracks. I don't want to be late for our meeting with White Feather."

Lara Newton was trying not to think about Skye Fargo.

She sat at a writing table in the quartermaster's office, having been left alone by the kindly, portly sergeant who was quite obviously nearing the end of a long military career. He had taken a fatherly—or perhaps it was grandfatherly—interest in accommodating her. The sergeant had assisted her in transporting her brother's effects from the storage room to this office so that she could inspect them in private. She had arranged Jeffrey's belongings so that his folded uniforms were near her chair, where she had gone through them expecting to find nothing. She was not disappointed. Upon the table before her were her brother's rifle, saber, and pistol. The quartermaster had explained, when she asked, that her brother had no doubt worn a personal sidearm on the ride into town with his fellow officers, the time he was last seen, as he was off duty. She didn't bother inspecting the saber or guns, but even as she turned her attention to a leather document pouch, she could not keep herself from thinking about Fargo. She thought of guns and weaponry as a hobby in Boston, not as a way of life, as with men like her brother and Fargo.

Would such a life become hers?

She opened the document pouch, which was secured by a clasped strap. She removed the packet she found inside the pouch.

Undoing a length of twine binding the sheaf of papers, she made a swift perusal of them, finding legal documents and official military correspondence including the orders assigning him to Fort Survival. Beneath these papers was a smaller packet of envelopes, not evident to her at first. These envelopes were each addressed, in identical feminine script, to her brother at his various posts, and each bore a Baltimore postmark.

She pondered the matter.

There was such a sense of finality about this, going through Jeffrey's things as if she were examining the effects of a dead man. She *was* thinking of Jeffrey in the past tense, and this realization made her stomach clench because, yes, she somehow *knew* in her deepest soul that her brother was no longer alive.

He had not deserted. Jeff never would do that. Yet it had been more than a month since he'd been heard from. Yes, he was dead.

Her eyes welled with tears, and she willed them to cease. The ache within her became determination.

She opened the envelopes and read their contents in order of their postmarks.

Jeff had never told her about Lilly. She was the daughter of Baltimore aristocracy, ostracized from society for her involvement in the theater. Lara could only imagine what her brother must have written, and what experiences these two must have shared, for the letters were in turn joyously romantic, lonely, reminiscent, full of happy anticipation and underpinned throughout by an abiding affection and love. The word *forever* appeared in each of her letters. Lilly was concerned for Jeff's safety in those letters addressed to his more dangerous duty assignments. From the dates, averaging twice a week, Lara determined that her brother had saved all of Lilly's letters. There was in them no mention of dark deeds, or references to mortal concern, nor any indication remotely related to trouble that Jeffrey may have gotten himself into or that may have gotten him killed.

She would contact Lilly. She would wait until after she'd learned what had truly happened to Jeffrey. Then she would thank the independent-minded young woman from Baltimore for bringing love into her brother's life.

She straightened the letters, preparing to return them to the pouch, knowing full well that Colonel Talbot, and more than likely at least one other officer, had already inspected the packet. Her elbow accidentally bumped the pouch from the table, knocking it to the floor. She leaned over in her chair, extending a hand to retrieve it, then paused, her fingertips extended.

Her eyes followed a tiny metal canister that had been secured within the weaving of the pouch's strap, but was knocked loose when the pouch hit the floor. The canister rolled to a stop beside her brother's boots.

She retrieved the canister, which was about a half inch long and the diameter of a twig. She twisted its ends in opposite directions, and the canister twisted. But her fingers were trembling with excitement, and the canister dropped to the table. She took a deep breath, willed her nerves to stay steady, attempted to open the canister again, and succeeded. She withdrew a tightly rolled piece of paper, which, when unrolled, was no more than one square inch. She scrutinized what was written on the paper in small hand, and for a moment she could not believe what she was seeing.

A wave of memories flashed across her mind.

*She and Jeffrey playing . . . she always behaving more like a boy than like a little girl, much to Mother's consternation. She and Jeffrey had even devised their own code for communicating, for no other reason than the childish fun of it. They would hide notes for each other as jokes or sometimes as private little brother-sister quarrels, conducted silently right in front of their stern parents, using notes they coded in case they were discovered. . . .*

Childish, yes.

And here she sat, staring down at the one-inch-square piece of hidden paper, staring at her brother's handwriting, a series of random letters and numbers that, even in this condensed form, made her know that she was looking at the same code they had used so long ago as children.

Oh, they'd kept it alive from time to time over the years, which is why she remembered it at all. When Jeffrey first left home for the academy, she had slipped a coded farewell note in with his personal effects, and he'd years later recalled his fondness at discovering it, keeping it near his heart through the ordeal of the first few rigorous weeks of officer training. And she had found a note from him after he left for Fort Survival, and that was the last time she'd seen him.

She carefully replaced the letters inside their proper envelopes, and left the envelopes as she had found them, beneath the sheaf of official documents. She looked again at the symbols on the piece of paper, then lifted her eyes to gaze thoughtfully at the blank wall opposite her.

Jeffrey had expected her to somehow find this note, or he had at least taken a long shot on that chance. He would know that his personal effects would eventually find their way to the family. He had wanted her to find the canister or he would never have written it in their childhood code from so long ago.

She studied the random digits and letters in her brother's hand, trying to remember the code and decipher what was written on the piece of paper.

This is what she had come West to find.

*A fine time for Fargo to be out playing scout for the colonel! He was supposed to be working for her!*

# 12

Fargo and Talbot rode into White Feather's camp at sunset.

The camp was a half-circle of teepees, pitched on a grassy knoll near a small creek. Trees stood like sentinels against the rouge sunset of the western sky. Nearby, ponies fed on the tall grass.

Fargo and Talbot rode past braves who regarded them with hostile stares. The braves held rifles. Though not aimed, the rifles were cocked, ready to be fired.

Birdcalls twittered from the trees. Birds dived at the winged bugs that flitted about, plentiful in the last rays of the day's sunlight. Children ran in laughing circles near where women prepared food.

There was a trio of braves who stood at the center teepee, where Fargo and Talbot reined in their horses. The brave in the center stepped forward. Fargo prepared to speak the man's language, but the brave spoke first.

"Down! Off your horses! Drop your guns."

Fargo dismounted without hesitation.

Talbot, continuing to keep an eye on Fargo for his cues, did likewise. He also unstrapped his gunbelt and rested it across the pommel of his saddle.

Talbot glanced at Fargo. "So they speak English. I won't be needing your services as a translator."

Fargo's knife was back in his boot. He said, "You still might be glad I'm along, Colonel, just the same."

"Could be," Talbot conceded dryly. "Never can tell." He eyed the brave. "You know who I am?"

The brave nodded. "White Feather waits for you." He held back the flap of the teepee, motioning for them to step inside.

Fargo went in first, having to stoop to enter. He stood as soon as he was inside and scanned the interior of the teepee even as Talbot followed him in.

The flap was left open. The trio of braves with rifles remained standing just outside.

Inside the teepee a fire crackled against the encroaching coolness of night.

White Feather sat cross-legged, puffing something aromatic from a long pipe. To either side of him, similarly cross-legged, sat a pair of tribal maidens, like bookends. The old chief remained an imposing figure. The full headdress he wore accentuated his stern visage. He motioned to a pair of blankets spread upon the ground, facing the fire, facing White Feather and the four maidens.

"Sit." It was an invitation, not a command.

Fargo and Talbot complied. Fargo did not much care for exposing his back to the open flap of the teepee, what with armed braves stationed outside there. On the other hand, he told himself as he assumed a cross-legged sitting position, at this point he was a dead man if White Feather wanted them dead. So he might as well take whatever advantage he could of this situation . . . and that most certainly included a visual appreciation of the four young lasses before him.

They were different in every way that human beings are different, and yet exact replicas in how they were clad in leather-fringe dresses that did nothing to conceal their full-breasted loveliness. Their long black air was braided, and they knelt submissively, doe eyes lowered modestly.

Colonel Talbot seated himself, cross-legged.

"Chief White Feather, it is good of you to travel to meet with me." He nodded cordially in Fargo's direction. "I understand that you know this man."

White Feather studied Fargo, and his aged eyes glinted, sharp as twin sword points.

"It has been a long time since our trails have crossed, Skye Fargo. Have your trails carried you to good places?"

Fargo shrugged mildly. "Some good, some not. It is good to see you again, my friend."

"And you, warrior brother." White Feather extended the pipe. "Smoke to our friendship."

Fargo accepted the pipe with both hands. "My pleasure to do so. Thank you."

He drew deeply. He passed the pipe to Talbot, who likewise drew before returning the pipe to White Feather, who set it down.

"I want this meeting," said White Feather, "so we can stop the uprising. There are renegades from my tribe, angry at the treaties that have been broken. They will not listen to the council elders." He locked eyes with Talbot. "And it is said that renegades have been blamed for raids by white-eyed desperadoes."

Fargo grunted. "Had some proof of that on our way in, matter of fact."

Talbot retained eye contact with White Feather.

"It is said that one man controls the raiders, the renegades from your tribe, and the desperadoes of whom you speak."

White Feather nodded. "I have heard this also,

122

whispered about the campfires like smoke on the wind."

Talbot's brow furrowed. "What do you mean?"

"He means that he's heard what we've heard—that one man is behind this uprising, for his own reward. Have you heard that spoken of, White Feather?"

"I have. This man, he sells rifles, ammunition, and, most important, he sells information, it is said, and for this they pay him."

Fargo nodded. "And most of the raiders behind this so-called uprising aren't working with each other."

Talbot leaned forward, regarding White Feather tenaciously. "Do you know who this man is?"

White Feather's eyes narrowed. "I do not." The tone of his reply was frosty.

Fargo leaned forward. "White Feather, Colonel Talbot knows that you are not this man we seek." He spoke earnestly, hurriedly. "You are the tribal elder most respected by my people, from the settlers to our leaders in the East. All know of White Feather's heroism, greatness in battle, and wisdom in time of peace."

Talbot leaned back appearing chastised, like an actor who has misread his cue.

"Of course. Fargo speaks far more eloquently than I. My apologies, Chief White Feather, if I have offended you."

White Feather reached for the pipe. "Let us smoke another bowl. We will stop this uprising. Enough of our people have died, yours and mine. The raiders must be stopped."

"Chief," said Fargo, "do you know the name Sanford?"

White Feather lowered, but did not set aside, the pipe.

"You people have such strange names. I learn your language, but do not understand your names. I am White Feather because when I came into this world, from the trees above my head there rustled a dove, and a white feather drifted down to touch my face. Or so the story is told. But Sanford? No, I do not know this name."

"Then since we have reached our understanding," said Talbot, "that is that we—your people and ours—will cooperate in settling this uprising, Fargo and I will be on our way, Chief White Feather. We thank you for your hospitality."

He started to stand.

White Feather lifted a hand. "But, Colonel, if our business here is complete and night has fallen, and as you men have implied, it is a dangerous ride back to the fort, will you not be my guests here for this night?"

Fargo glanced at Talbot. "It would be a show of friendship to accept the chief's hospitality, sir."

Talbot nodded promptly. "You're quite right, of course. Thank you, White Feather. Fargo and I have our bedrolls. We will pitch out camp at the edge of your camp."

White Feather raised his hand. "Please, no. I offer you each a teepee of your own for the night." He indicated the maidens on either side of him. "And I offer to each of you one of my wives for warmth against the night chill, and for your own pleasure."

"And for hers, let's hope." Fargo found himself smiling. "Chief, that is mighty hospitable of you."

He caught the eye of the last girl on his left. She covered her giggle with her small, dancing brown fingers and looked away, chattering merrily, bawdily, with the other wives until White Feather lifted his hand, this time an abrupt, commanding gesture, and their feminine chatter ceased.

The old chief looked at Talbot. "And you, Colonel? It is my wish that you be made to feel most welcomed here."

The colonel cleared his throat, and thumbed his cropped white mustache. "Er, you are most hospitable, Chief White Feather, I must say." He was clearly uncomfortable. "But I am also obliged to say that, unlike our footloose friend Fargo here, I have pledged myself to one woman only. I have a wife and children in Kansas City."

White Feather nodded. "Kansas City. I have heard of this place. And it is a good man, Colonel, who honors his vows."

Talbot stood.

"And so you will excuse me then, I trust. Fargo, I'll expect you to be saddled up and ready to head out at dawn."

Fargo had not been able to resume eye contact with the comely wife on the end, but knew she was aware that his eyes had been upon her.

"Yes, sir."

Talbot extended a hand to White Feather. "Chief, thank you for being a man of honesty and truth."

They shook hands.

"Peace will come to this land," said White Feather. "We are entrusted to make this happen, you and I, Colonel Talbot," His eyes and visage warmed as he regarded the women who sat around the fire. "But for this night, we are entrusted with our oneness with the harmony of man and woman."

"I envy you the closeness of your loved ones," said

Talbot. "For this soldier, tonight will be a sound sleep under the stars, knowing satisfaction in what has been settled between us. Routes of communication must be established, but for now, good night to you."

They nodded to each other, and Talbot left the teepee.

Fargo reclined into an even more comfortable position upon the blanket, stretching his length closer to the fire . . . and closer to the young woman who'd caught his eye and was suddenly pretending to be ever so submissive and shy.

Darkness had fallen beyond the open flap of the tent. The armed braves remained, positioned just outside. Inside, the fire's flickering warmth—and the presence of four attractive, desirable females—created a comfortable, yet arousing, ambiance.

Fargo nodded to the pipe, still held by the chief.

"And, uh, White Feather . . ."

After smoking the ceremonial pipe with White Feather, Fargo stood and extended a hand to the wife of his choice. Her name was Spring Flower, and she rose willingly, with a femininely inscrutable smile upon her lovely face. Her brown eyes glittered in the campfire light, as unreadable as her smile.

Ordinarily, Fargo was opposed to sleeping with married women. But since it was culturally permitted and the chief *did* have three other wives, Fargo figured he could certainly afford to spare one for the night.

Not to mention that the lady herself seemed willing enough.

White Feather nodded his unspoken blessing to Fargo. Taking his hand, Spring Flower guided him from the teepee. The three remaining beauties commenced cooing and fawning over the old tiger.

Fargo chuckled, and allowed himself to be led to the next teepee over.

There was no sign of Talbot, and he figured that was just as well. Although entranced by Spring Flower's considerable charm, he did not let her charms dull his awareness of his surroundings.

The chief's sentries remained at their posts, positioned outside White Feather's teepees and at outcrops of land.

There was the aura of *woman* inside this teepee, in its appointments and muted candlelight. There was a thrown-down bearskin rug, upon which Spring Flower threw herself with an earthy giggle of enthusiasm, his first real indication that she was less submissive that she pretended to be. *But then,* the thought came to him, *what woman isn't?*

She took him by the hand and tugged him down with her and he allowed himself to sprawl with her across the caressing, sensual comfort of the bear fur.

They embraced, kissing torridly, and he ran his hands across the curves beneath her fringe dress. Her naturally upthrust breasts mashed against his chest. He buried his nostrils in the feral scent of her black hair, and his roaming hands cupped her from behind. She shuddered, and determinedly clawed her way to get atop him, the tigress within her wholly revealed. She crushed her pelvis to his, and his manhood grew hard.

Then she lowered her mouth to his erection.

He ran his fingers through her long, coal-black hair. Her head bobbed and almost immediately she brought him to a climax.

He embraced her then, her body curving on its side to snuggle in against him. She rested her head on his chest, but one of her hands remained touching his flaccid, spent member. She purred, content because they both knew that she had temporarily cooled his ardor only so that when he became hard again, he would remain so for a considerably longer time, to give her more pleasure.

After this tender time passed, her fingers began stroking his manhood back to life, gently, teasingly at first, the tips of her fingers gliding along its underside, to encircle its head with squeezing strokes . . . before releasing him to begin again. Before much more of this, his member took shape and when it did she knelt and used her mouth again, but this time stopped when he was good and hard.

She pasted her body to his, so he could again run his hands over her hips and thighs, one of his palms sliding the hem of her fringed dress up across vibrant, brown, muscular flesh, the skirt bunching around her hips. His erection brushed through her thatch of coal-black pubic hair before encountering her moist mound. Spring Flower moaned, and arched her hips.

Fargo lowered his face to the bushy, musky place between her legs, and began kissing what he found there. She moaned some more. Her hips bucked and twisted against his face when he found her spot and began flicking his tongue. She squealed. Her climax was of hips bouncing and her head whipping from side to side, her outstretched hands grasping like claws at the bearskin.

When her spasms and her moaning subsided into pleasurable cooing, Fargo drew himself to an upright position between her spread legs, his head and shoulders thrown back, his manhood extending before him like a pointing pole. He gripped her by her hips and tugged forcefully, though not roughly, and Spring Flower squealed again when the length of his shaft sank into her and he pulled her hips flush to his. He grasped each of her calves and flung one leg over each of his shoulders. Steadying her in this manner and with his hands holding her hips, he commenced pumping her hard and fast. She gasped with intensifying pleasure with his every thrust. Her shapely breasts, beneath the fringe dress top, bounced, and this time Fargo and Spring Flower crested a crescendo of sexual climax together.

# 13

Like many veteran scouts, Fargo knew the sign language of the Plains tribes, and enough of the tribes' spoken languages to generally get by in most disputes or social interactions.

This allowed for ample postcoital conversation between Fargo and Spring Flower. But Fargo made sure that his gun belt with the holstered Colt, his Henry, and the ammunition pouch were close at hand—just in case. They'd returned his weapons to him upon his leaving the chief's teepee with Spring Flower, and had informed him that Colonel Talbot had also regained possession of his weapons.

Spring Flower threw another log on the fire. They sipped water from a deerskin pouch, and she returned to his arms. The fur blanket was wrapped about them.

"You are magnificent, Skye Fargo."

Her breath, as she whispered, brushed his chest hairs. He felt so good he had a little bit of the devil in him.

"As magnificent as the old chief?"

She paused. "You ask me to speak of my husband after we have just made love?"

He mentally kicked himself in the butt. He reached down and gave her butt an affectionate pat.

"Sorry, hon. Just feeling fresh. You're magnificent too, beautiful Spring Flower."

She raised her head to gaze into his eyes. "And you are gentle for a man who has killed. Men who kill carry an aura about them—did you know that?"

"I know it."

"If their violent acts do not bring demons to them, such men live life with more strength than is found in those who are not warriors."

"You know much for a woman of such tender years." He meant it as a mild tease.

"I am the wife of White Feather." Her response was dead serious. "My chief possesses that gentle strength of the warrior, of which I speak. You may jest, but here is your answer. Making love with you is like making love with my husband. Skye Fargo, you make love like one of *us*." Now it was her tone that sparkled with mischief. "And you do know that your people call my people savages?"

"Some do." He felt an ear-to-ear grin slide across his stubbly face, and knew that he must have looked dopey as all get-out. "So you're telling me that old Skye makes love like a savage, eh? Reckon I've been called worse."

Strands of her coal-black hair laced across his lips, titillating his nostrils with the scent of her.

"When I say that you make love like my husband," she said, "it is the supreme compliment."

He hugged her closer. The pliant heat of her breasts pressed against his side. "I accept it as such."

She purred. "You have the savage in you when you make love, yes, and you have that manner I have felt only with a paleface. I mean to say that there is only one other white man that I ever, that is . . ." She hesi-

131

tated. "He was a soldier. He came here like you with Colonel Talbot."

Quickly as that, the spell was broken.

Fargo couldn't bring himself to release this delicious feminine bundle in his arms. Without releasing her, he propped himself up and looked into her eyes.

"Spring Flower, what was the soldier's name?"

"His name was Jeffrey. He was . . . is it called a lieutenant?"

"It is. How did you come to be Jeffrey's lover?"

"First you wish to speak of my husband, and now of Jeffrey. I was offered to him by White Feather," she said, eye to eye, "as I was offered to you."

"As you were to me," he repeated. "How do you feel about that, Spring Flower?"

A rebellious flicker sparkled in her irises. "You would think me wicked."

"Go on, tell me anyway."

"When I see a bird take wing across the open sky, I feel . . . I feel *that* is the nature of *my* spirit. Do you understand? I liked very much being with Jeffrey. He was an artful lover, though more"—she searched for the word—"tame than you. He was not a savage. But it is true, I enjoyed pleasure with him, as I have with you."

"You're like a free bird," he said. "I'm surprised that's not your name. A free spirit." He thought of the other woman he had considered in those terms during the past forty-eight hours. Lara. He was accustomed to taking his pleasure where he found it when offered the charms of those ladies he encountered on the trail of his life. "Please," he asked Spring Flower, "tell me about Jeffrey."

"Have I not told you the most intimate things that a woman can tell about a man? For one night, he and I were lovers. Here, in this teepee, on this knoll, on a moonlit night much like this. This is a favorite spot of White Feather's, to make camp and hold meetings."

"You said the lieutenant, Jeffrey, came here with Colonel Talbot."

She nodded. "It was when the uprising first began. The colonel and the chief were suspicious of each other. Their distrust remained unsettled until tonight. There was strain between them that night, and yet as a gesture, I was . . . I was offered to Jeffrey." She studied Fargo anew, her head cocked slightly. "Are you jealous, Skye? I *am* another man's wife."

He chuckled and delivered her another affectionate spank on the rump.

"No, honey, I've got a reason to be curious. Has White Feather brought you back to this place since that night?"

"Not until this night."

"What happened after you and Jeffrey made love?"

She frowned. "The colonel had retired to beyond our camp, as he has tonight. But on that night, after Lieutenant Jeffrey and I made love, Colonel Talbot came to stand outside the teepee and summoned Jeffrey to join him. Jeffrey quickly clothed himself. He kissed me good-bye, and went to join the colonel."

"Wonder if I should expect a visit from the colonel tonight?"

"No, that's not what I am saying," she said tartly. "Colonel Talbot would have been here before now if it was to be tonight as it was on that night. Your lovemaking, Skye, lasted." Again the hesitation of maidenly modesty. "You have far more stamina."

"Uh, Spring Flower, that's not what I want to talk about. Did you see what happened after the lieutenant met the colonel that night?"

"Yes. As I say, it was a night of the big moon, as tonight. I do not know your language, and so I could not understand what they said when they spoke to each other just outside of my teepee. But it seemed to me that the colonel asked Jeffrey to go with him along a game trail that leads down from this knoll. I thought that the colonel wanted to show Lieutenant Jeffrey something."

"What happened then?"

"After they left, I fell asleep. The hour was late." A peculiar sadness entered her tone of voice. "I never saw Jeffrey again. At dawn the next morning, we left here as White Feather had intended. I heard him say that the pony soldiers left before the dawn."

Fargo gave her rump a parting, affectionate pat. *A wonderful rump, and a great romp!* But now it was time to get back to business. He couldn't think about lovemaking anymore, even if he'd wanted to, until after he followed through on the ideas that were rapidly shuffling into place in his mind like the pieces of a puzzle.

"I'd like you to show me this trail where you saw Lieutenant Jeffrey and the colonel for the last time."

"Has something bad happened to Lieutenant Jeffrey? I don't understand."

"I'm just beginning to," said Fargo.

He released her, rose to his feet, and was clothed within a minute, including the cartridge belt around his waist, the Colt low on his hip.

She didn't bother wearing anything, which suited Fargo just fine. When they emerged from her teepee, moonlight limned her every curve, and made blacker the hair falling upon her shoulders.

The world was sleeping, or seemed to be. Night insects chirped. A night breeze carried with it the scent of mesquite. Moonlight etched everything in silver; the teepees, boulders, foliage, and trees.

She pointed. "There."

Fargo couldn't help but spend a fleeting instant admiring the effect the pointing motion had in swaying her shapely breasts, then he tugged his eyes away to gaze in the direction in which she was pointing.

A game trail was discernible cutting through high grass, leading out of sight.

He gave her a hug and delivered a kiss to the top of her head. "Thank you, Spring Flower. And thanks for what you shared with me tonight."

"I wish to thank you, Skye Fargo, for the pleasure you brought to me. Tonight my heart truly soared, like that of a bird. Let me go with you, down the trail."

He chuckled. "No, the cactus would stick you all over that pretty little body of yours, and I don't think your husband would approve of that." He brought his lips close to her ear. He whispered. "And I want you to do something for me."

"Yes, what do you wish, my white savage? Anything."

"Go back to White Feather."

She blinked, not understanding. "But of course."

"And tell him that I said to remember Missionary Wells. Can you remember that for me?"

"Of course. Missionary Wells."

"Tell him right now."

"I will." She started to slide her arms around his neck, to draw her nakedness to him for a farewell kiss. She received another kiss to the top of her tangled coal-black hair.

"Spring Flower, good night."

And he was gone.

He heard the rustle of movement from behind him, indicating that she was heeding his request.

He started down the vaguely defined, twisty game trail that curled down through knee-high grass. He moved through the night with a stealth that did not disturb or silence the peeping insects. He unleathered the Colt, hoping that the faint click of its hammer being cocked reached his ears alone.

The terrain spread out for untold miles below and beyond him, like a silver sea beneath the white moon, the undulating terrain of sparse vegetation like vast rolling waves. Closer to him, the game trail curved from sight around a mass of boulders.

He neared the boulders and smelled the faintest scent of human presence on the breeze, discernible to a man used to the solitude of such places. He drew up short and heard the barely discernible whispering of a male and a female voice. He altered his course and completed his final approach of the boulders from below, not from the direction of the knoll.

Lara Newton, and the man she stood conversing with, were distinctly perceptible in the light of the moon. Lara wore riding britches and a jacket. In the moonlight her blond hair looked snow-white.

The man next to her was a strapping, square-jawed fellow wearing a U.S. Cavalry uniform. The moonlight shone off his lieutenant's bars. They were examining and discussing, between themselves, a battered U.S. Cavalry hat, and they both looked up when Fargo stepped from behind a boulder, revealing his presence. The cavalryman relinquished his hold on the hat and started to reach for his buttoned-down flap holster.

Fargo lifted the Colt so its muzzle was aimed at this lieutenant's midriff.

"You know you're about to commit suicide, don't you, Lieutenant, even if I am the one who pulls the trigger? I advise you to stay that hand."

The soldier's hand hovered near his holster.

Lara stepped between them.

"Skye Fargo," she started to introduce him in her proper Bostonian manner, "this is—"

"I'll take it from here, ma'am," said the cavalryman. His eyes were on Fargo. "The name's Carruthers. I'd advise you, sir, to lower your weapon."

"Lieutenant Carruthers," said Lara, "is"—her voice faltered—"was my brother's . . . my brother's replacement. Skye, he's been most helpful to me. I think I know what happened to Jeffrey."

Fargo lowered his pistol, but did not holster it. "So do I." He nodded to the battered cavalry hat she was holding. "That was your brother's hat."

"His initials are on the sweatband." Her voice quavered sorrowfully.

"I'm sorry, Lara. The colonel killed Jeff. I just learned a few minutes ago that Talbot brought your brother here to meet with White Feather. Talbot has to have civilians working for him, gunslingers to do the strong-arm stuff. They came back after White Feather left, and removed the body. They must have overlooked the hat."

"When I went through Jeffrey's things," whispered Lara, "I found something he left for me, something he hoped I would find, and in case anyone else saw it he wrote it in a code we used as children. I had to think for a while but when I remembered how we did it, that message translated into only two words: 'Commander corrupt.'"

Fargo nodded. "He was right. There are missing

137

pieces, but the Army can put that together. I've got the general picture."

Carruthers's lantern jaw jutted. "And what would that be? I've got a column riding in, Fargo, about a half hour behind me. I rode ahead to place the colonel under arrest. I've allowed Miss Newton to accompany me since she has been so instrumental in this. We were reconnoitering the area when this hat caught our eye."

Fargo said, "Over the months it must have blown from wherever it was concealed from the ones who removed the body." He said to Lara, "We're not going to find any trace of your brother, not if Talbot wanted the deserter charge against Jeff to stick."

Lara held her brother's hat to her as it was a treasure to be fiercely guarded.

"That does make sense," she said in a quiet, even voice. "I went to Lieutenant Carruthers and told him about Jeffrey's coded message. I convinced him to assist me."

"It didn't take much convincing," said Carruthers. "A woman travels across the country to a hostile frontier, to find out what happened to a family member . . . well, you're inclined to give her the benefit of the doubt."

The lieutenant had become smitten with the lady from Boston, as any healthy male would, Fargo noted.

"We searched the files in the colonel's office," said Lara. "Skye, he's been diverting arms shipments and selling them for personal gain!"

Fargo nodded. "That's why he killed your brother. Somehow Jeffrey caught on. You told me he was inquisitive."

"I telegraphed Washington as soon as Miss Newton's suspicions were verified," said Carruthers. "I also learned that the colonel had ordered a column to leave the fort in the middle of the night to travel with a Gatling gun, with orders to wipe out this encampment. The colonel left word that White Feather was behind the uprising in the territory, and Talbot was risking his life to lure White Feather into position for an attack."

"And I would be cut down with everyone else in the camp," said Fargo. "The colonel knew that."

"I rescinded those orders, of course," said Carruthers. He unholstered his revolver.

"Talbot engineered the uprising," said Fargo. "He's making money selling guns and ammunition, and he's taking a cut of the raiders' loot. Because he's the one source that supplies rifles to all of them, he knows everything about them. That's how he put his organization together. He has it so well organized, one of his own gangs captured us and almost killed their own boss without even knowing it! Talbot didn't say a word because he figured we could get out. He didn't know how much I knew, and he wanted to lead me along."

Carruthers scanned the surrounding gloom. "Lara, I mean Miss Newton, told me about Sanford in El Paso. And where is Colonel Talbot now?"

"That's what *I* was reconnoitering to find out," said Fargo. "I suggest that we locate and apprehend him without further delay."

"Too late," a voice rasped from the darkness behind Carruthers. "I've found *you*."

The murkiness behind Carruthers suddenly shifted, and he was jerked backward, off his feet. Even as he tracked his Colt in that direction, Fargo saw the arm around Carruthers's chest, yanking forcefully, and a fast sideways slashing motion, then the glimmer of a knife blade in the moonlight. There was a slicing sound and a death rattle as Carruthers coughed blood. Then Fargo heard the thud of a body falling.

Lara cried out in dismay.

Fargo fired twice at the crackle of branches in the darkness behind where Carruthers had dropped. In the golden muzzle-flash of gunfire, he saw Talbot dart at Lara from behind. The colonel's uniform looked sharply pressed, even in the moonlight.

Moonlight danced across the knife blade that he raised to Lara's jugular vein, using his other arm to clasp her body against his, ahead of him, like a human shield. He snickered in her ear.

"This is how I killed your brother, little lady. That's why no shot was heard in White Feather's camp that night." Then he snarled at Fargo from behind Lara's head of blond curls. "Now drop that gun you're aiming at me, scout, or I'll slit her throat."

# 14

With Talbot utilizing Lara as a human shield, Fargo lowered his pistol and held it at his side. He saw the darkness shift soundlessly behind Talbot.

Fargo said, "Have you got him, White Feather?"

Talbot snickered. "I can't believe you're trying that old ruse, Fargo, a man of your supposed ingenuity and resourcefulness."

Then Talbot gasped, and Fargo knew this would be because the old chief had eased in behind the colonel, as soundlessly as the colonel had eased in behind Carruthers. The chief would be holding a rifle muzzle pressed to the base of Talbot's spine. White Feather and Fargo had once rode together and this was how they'd rescued a tribal elder held hostage by White Feather's enemies, once upon a time at a place called Missionary Wells.

"I am here." The chief's baritone rumbled from the darkness like the voice of a god. "You will drop your knife, Colonel, or killing this woman will be your final act. Step away from her."

The knife clattered to the ground. Talbot stepped away from Lara.

She hurried to Fargo's side.

White Feather appeared from the shadows. He was alone. He wore buckskins and a full headdress. He held an Army-issue repeating rifle. Talbot faced them.

Some of Carruthers's blood had splattered across the front of his spotless uniform; dark splotches appeared on the fabric. White Feather aimed his rifle at Talbot.

Fargo said, "I'm mighty disappointed in you, Colonel."

Talbot snorted derisively. "I'm six months from retirement. Am I supposed to retire on a soldier's pay and live out my days a pitiable pauper in an old soldier's home? I don't have a wife and children. I've got a string of whores in fancy hotels in El Paso. I got used to the good life, scout. Once you get that taste, you don't want to give it up."

"Name's Fargo," said Fargo.

"Your name is shit," Talbot hissed. "I've hated your guts ever since that day on the Piedra. I could have been a general by now."

"From what I've been told," put in Lara, "you could have been dead."

"I'd rather have died that day," said Talbot in a strange, different voice. Then the belligerence returned. "But I didn't. I was branded a bad officer and had to start over from the bottom, and look at me, commanding a squalid fort when I should be at a desk in Washington, staying at the Ritz with my mistresses."

White Feather said, "Fargo, let me kill him now. He should die by one of *his* rifles."

Fargo thought of the "death by poetic justice" of Sanford, killed by that ricochet at the El Paso Metal Works.

"No," he said. "I let him bring me this far after I started having my doubts about him because I wanted something tangible that can be used against him. He's going to pay, White Feather, but I want it to be before a military court."

White Feather lowered his rifle.

"I have heard what was said." He indicated Carruthers's body, at their feet. "I regret that I was not able to save this man's life." He turned to Lara, his eyes glinting like twin sword points even in the moonlight. "Believe me, young woman, when I say that the colonel told me your brother had ridden off ahead that morning, after his murder. I had no idea the thing had happened."

"I believe you, of course," said Lara. "And I understand." Her back was rigid. She glared at Talbot, but spoke to White Feather. "I owe you my life."

Fargo didn't take his eyes from Talbot, either. "Chief, you and your folks had better break camp, if you want my advice. In time they'll ask you to bring Spring Flower in to testify about what she knows."

"Spring Flower?" asked Lara, a frown in her voice.

"Later," said Fargo. And to White Feather, he said, "What do you say, Chief?"

"I will speak to the tribal council," said White Feather. "I will make sure to tell them that you, the Trailsman, have brought this uprising to an end. The bandits and renegades will go when the guns no longer come cheap to them and there is no one to provide them with information. Good-bye, Fargo. We will meet again."

"So long, Chief. And, uh, thank you for your hospitality. Tell Spring Flower that I said good-bye."

And White Feather was no longer there. Moments later, activity began stirring atop the knoll.

Talbot sneered at Fargo. "Damn Indian lover."

"Only the decent ones," said Fargo. "Kind of the way I feel about white folks."

"Well ain't we high and mighty. So what are you going to do with me now, scout, shoot me down?"

Lara left Fargo's side, to retrieve Carruthers's pistol. She returned to his side, and aimed the revolver at Talbot.

"I'll be glad to," she said coldly, "for what you did to my brother, you piece of snake shit."

Fargo stretched out his free hand and smoothly lowered her arm. "All of a sudden you don't sound like a lady from Boston."

"I don't understand," she said, "about Jeff riding off from his fellow officers on their way to Shantytown."

"My guess is the colonel told your brother it was a secret mission to get White Feather," said Fargo. "You were planning to blame White Feather for the uprising all along, weren't you, Colonel? Jeff rode along, just like I did, because he was trying to get more on what you were up to. Unfortunately for Jeff, he somehow tipped his hand. That's why you lured him away from the camp and murdered him. If it weren't for Lara here, the deserter story would have been good enough to fool everyone."

"So tell me, scout." There was a permanent sneer in Talbot's expression, and in his voice. "Go ahead and brag. How did you arrive at this brilliant deduction?"

"It just now fell into place for me," said Fargo. "The pieces of the puzzle came at me one at a time, then added up. Colonel, when Lara and I first rode in, you told me there was no clue about who was behind the uprising. But even a whore in Shantytown had heard rumors that it was a white man running the show."

"A whore in Shantytown?" asked Lara.

"She told me this man controlled the gangs without them working with each other," said Fargo. "But you didn't say anything to me about that, sir, and when I did hear about it, that seemed sort of strange. I hear these raiders know where to strike and when and where to avoid the Army patrols. That was another mark against you, because you could do that easy if you wanted to, sir. But I kept trying to give you the benefit of the doubt because I figured you *were* a good soldier."

"To hell with you, Fargo."

"During our ride here, you didn't tell me that Lara's brother had ridden here with you once before, when you damn well knew that was the reason I had come to Fort Survival. When I found that out, I knew it was you, Colonel. And I reckon that about sums it up. Like I said, I'm mighty disappointed in you, sir."

"And like I said," snarled Talbot, "to hell with you. I haven't heard anything that would even remotely stand up in a court martial."

Lara laughed without humor. "You mean, other than you holding a knife to my throat and admitting that it was the same method you'd used to kill my brother?"

Horse hooves and the shuffling of feet, a general sense of movement, could be heard from the knoll as White Feather's people withdrew into the night.

Talbot guffawed.

"You, Miss Newton, are delusional and overwrought by the fact that your brother was a deserter." He nodded in the direction of the receding sounds. "An Indian savage is your only witness, and he *is* behind the uprising. As a career officer, my word will hold up against his and that of a scout's in any court-martial in this man's Army."

"Damn, sir," said Fargo. "You make a mighty good case for me plunking a bullet into your brain pan right now. But fact is, that column of Lieutenant Carruthers's ought to be here anytime. A couple of blood-suckers like you and Sanford would never trust each other. When they dig, the Army will find bank records concerning the transfer of funds. When the El Paso–Fort Survival connection is made, you'll go behind bars. Not even the old soldier's home for you, sir."

"All because of a low-life scout."

Talbot's voice was equal parts resignation and fury, and he unexpectedly lunged sideways, reaching for his sidearm. Fargo lost sight of him as the blackness of night swallowed Talbot.

"Damn," said Fargo. "Lara, get back. Stay down."

She too vanished from his sight fast enough to indicate that she hadn't needed to be told.

He stepped back into the shadows opposite where the colonel had left the clearing just as the flash, thunder, and coppery lightning of gunfire spat from there once, twice. Bullets buzzed through shrubbery nowhere near where Fargo crouched, and he hoped Lara was staying low. The colonel would be on the move, trying to make his escape, so Fargo fanned off six rapid shots in a straight line, a tight pattern that sprayed across the clearing. There was a single gunshot, from a point considerably to the right of Talbot's preceding fire, and this muzzle flash indicated a bullet fired at the ground, unaimed, the gun triggered reflexively. There came the sound of a falling body.

Silence.

"Be careful," Lara called. "It could be a trap."

Fargo snapped his Colt's cylinder into place after reloading with fresh cartridges. "I'll find out," he said.

She said something that he didn't hear because he was soundlessly withdrawing from his position, circling the clearing, staying away from shafts of moonlight that just barely delineated shrubbery and scrub oak.

A few feet beyond the body of Carruthers, he found Talbot's corpse. One of his bullets had caught the colonel high in the chest.

Fargo relieved the corpse of its revolver and cartridge belt. He stepped into the clearing. Lara appeared and even though she still held Carruthers's pistol, Fargo had the incongruously strange sensation that he was witnessing a gorgeous vision materialize in the moonlight like an angel; a shapely angel, her figure encased in riding britches and jacket.

He handed her Talbot's cartridge belt. She buckled it around her shapely waist, the colonel's pistol riding on one hip, Carruthers's pistol, the gun-butt forward, inside the belt at her other hip. *A heavily armed angel*, thought Fargo. And through it all, she'd never released her hold on her brother's battered cavalry hat, which she held delicately under her arm. She sighed as she cinched the gunbelt.

"Well, I guess we know what happened to Jeffrey."

"I reckon so. I am sorry, Lara."

"You needn't be." Aloofness crept into her tone and demeanor. "You'll be receiving the second half of your retainer as soon as we reach El Paso, and I shall return to Boston to tell my family, and the Army, the truth. My brother was not a deserter. He died in the honorable service of his country. Yes, a fitting end to this adventure, I think."

The Ovaro and her dun materialized, stepping expectantly into the clearing.

In the distance hoofbeats could be heard approaching from the direction of Fort Survival—the opposite direction taken by White Feather—galloping inexorably closer, presently about a half mile out, Fargo estimated. The rattle of sabers carried across the open expanse of prairie.

"That will be Lieutenant Carruthers's column of soldier boys."

Lara stared at Carruthers's body.

"He was a good man. He gave his life."

Fargo swung into the saddle.

"Right now, I suggest we light a shuck out of here. We'll come forward and give the Army everything we know at *our* convenience. I've spent enough time around the military not to want to get involved in their way of handling things. I suggest we light out for El Paso, *pronto*."

Lara held the cavalry hat in her hands now, staring down at it.

"You're right. Poor Jeffrey. Very well, let's be gone."

She swung into her saddle, and Fargo could not help but admire the trim lines of her legs, whose muscular shapeliness was not concealed by her britches; and, speaking of muscular shapeliness in britches, his brief glimpse in the moonlight of her rump as she mounted her steed was a sight he'd remember fondly if he lived to be an old man.

It occurred to him that, with his job for her completed, and her already speaking of returning to Boston, he was not that far from bidding a likely permanent farewell to the lady from Boston who had so recently offered him her most intimate charms, back there at Sanford's mansion in El Paso when he had been too damn busy with other matters to take her up on her offer. He liked the way Lara Newton combined the class of Boston high society with the resilient survival skills of a Western woman born and bred. She was a rare one, and Fargo decided that it was high time that he made up for lost time.

They galloped away from the knoll, taking a southerly course. The prairie stretched before them, all silver and shadow beneath the stars.

Fargo called over to her as they rode, side by side. "Uh, Lara. Maybe after we get back to El Paso, we could—"

"There *are* two questions I still have," she called back.

"And what would those be?"

"Who is Spring Flower, and what's the name of that whore in Shantytown?"

"Uh."

"You had your chance with me, mister. And I would have been the best you ever had," she called to him, the brazen defiance—a challenge?—in her voice discernible to him even through the clatter of their horses' hooves. "But you'd rather spend your time with sporting girls and Indian maidens."

She coaxed more speed out of the dun, which bolted her into a considerable lead ahead of Fargo.

He watched her gallop off across undulating folds of moon-shadow, charting her progress for a while, allowing her some distance to let off steam though he kept her in sight.

"Well, there's always a chance," he told the Ovaro.

He coaxed the stallion into a gallop, and gave chase.

# LOOKING FORWARD!

**The following is the opening
section from the next novel in the exciting
*Trailsman* series from Signet:**

**THE TRAILSMAN #244
PACIFIC POLECATS**

---

*The Pacific Northwest 1861—Hatred comes in many
guises, and death strikes when least expected.*

Skye Fargo was five miles from Seattle when he first
became aware that he was being shadowed. A sense
of unease came over him, and without being obvious
he scanned the thick timber through which his Ovaro
stallion was passing. Nothing moved amid the Dou-
glas firs, but Fargo knew better than to ignore his in-
tuition. *Something* was out there. Something that
didn't want him to know it was there.

Fargo mentally catalogued the possibilities. Griz-
zlies were common along the Pacific coast, but he
hadn't seen signs of grizzly for hours. Mountain lions
were also abundant, but they generally left humans
alone unless bothered. Wolves were only a threat
when they were starving, and there was plenty of

game about. That left two likely candidates: roving Indians or white bandits.

For almost a decade the Yakima tribe had been on the warpath. But not all that long ago they had been defeated in a fierce battle and ever since had been as peaceable as lambs. In any event, the Yakima lived farther east. The nearby coast tribes, so far as Fargo knew, were friendly.

That reduced Fargo's list to a single possibility; the skulkers in the undergrowth had to be whites. And whoever they were, if they were going to such extraordinary lengths not to be detected, they had to be up to no good.

Fargo casually switched the Ovaro's reins to his left hand and lowered his right hand to the smooth butt of his Colt. For the next several minutes his lake-blue eyes continually probed the brush from under the brim of his low-slung hat, but he saw nothing to justify his suspicion.

Then, twenty yards west of the rutted trail, a man on horseback appeared, a big slab of beef in buckskins similar to Fargo's. An unkempt beard sprawled across his barrel chest, and a tangled mane of hair framed his coldly sinister face. Cradled in the crook of the man's left elbow was a Sharps rifle.

Fargo nodded, but the man didn't return the gesture. Watching him, Fargo almost missed the second horseman, a gangly specimen in a faded flannel shirt who was east of the trail about the same distance. The second rider wore a floppy hat and was partial to a Remington revolver worn butt-forward on his left hip.

As the Ovaro went by, the pair kneed their mounts and came up behind him. Shifting in the saddle, Fargo kept them in sight as he rounded a slight bend. The stallion snorted, and he swung around to find two more horsemen up ahead in a small clearing. Both were cut from the same coarse cloth as the first pair. On the right was a tall drink of water in a broad-brimmed hat with a high crown, a style popular with cowhands from the northern plains. His vest, chaps and spurs were additional proof he once made a living herding cattle. On the left was a runt who looked like a weasel with slick greasy hair.

It was the runt who smiled thinly, held up a dirty hand, and declared, "Hold on there, mister. We'd like a word with you."

Fargo was inclined to ride on by, but he didn't want the four of them at his back. If they were up to no good—and they likely were—they wouldn't hesitate to shoot him in the back given the chance. He brought the pinto to a stop side-on so he could keep all four in sight. "What can I do for you gents?" he asked amiably enough, even as his right hand tightened on the Colt and his whole body tensed.

The weasel grinned, baring a mouth with more yellow teeth than white ones. "My name is Kellim. Would yours happen to be Fargo? Skye Fargo?"

Fargo's mind raced faster than a bullet. He was sure he'd never set eyes on Kellim or any of the others before. So how was it they knew him? More importantly, how had they known he was taking that particular trail at that particular time? "What if it is?" he asked.

Kellim's grin widened. "We hear you're bound for the settlement up yonder. But you're not going to get there. You're going to turn around and light a shuck back to San Francisco."

Fargo's curiosity climbed. Only one person in all of Washington Territory knew where he had been when he received the urgent message that brought him north. "Why would I want to do that?"

"Because you aim to live to a ripe told age."

"I take that as a threat," Fargo casually commented. The other three were watching him with the piercing concentration of hawks ready to swoop in for the kill.

"Take it any damn way you please, mister," Kellim responded, "just so you do as we want. Otherwise, there will be hell to pay."

The man with the busy beard leveled his rifle. "And you don't want that to happen, not unless you're partial to breathin' dirt."

Four against one weren't odds to Fargo's liking, but he wasn't about to turn tail. Not with so much at stake. He saw that the rider with the Remington had it half-drawn, and the cowpoke's right hand hovered inches from a Smith and Wesson. "Who put you up to this?" he stalled.

"Who claimed anyone did?" was Kellim's cagey retort. Around his narrow waist was buckled a Merwin and Hulbert open-top Army revolver which he made no attempt to bring to bear. "Do everyone a favor and light out."

"Right this second," stressed the man with the Sharps.

Life, Fargo had found, was much like poker. When a person was dealt a bad hand, the smart thing to do was fold and wait for better cards. So it was best if he did exactly as the quartet wanted. But what if they had been hired to kill him, not merely scare him off? What was to stop them from putting four or five slugs into him as he rode off? "I know a stacked deck when I see one," he said to make them think he had been cowed. "If you want me to leave, that's what I'll do."

"I'm glad you're so obliging," Kellim responded, smiling. "Makes it a lot easier all around."

"That's me, all right," Fargo said. "Obliging as hell." So saying, he lashed his reins and slapped his legs against the Ovaro and the stallion bolted straight toward the slab of beef holding the Sharps. The man tried to raise it to his shoulder but Fargo was on top of him before he could. The Ovaro's shoulder slammed into the man's bay and the bay suffered the worst of the impact. Nickering and rearing, it forced its owner to cling on or be unseated.

In the bat of an eye Fargo was among the trees, Kellim's shout ringing in his ears. "After him, you jackasses! If he gives us the slip we won't get the rest of the money!"

Heavy hooves pounded in Fargo's wake. He ducked low over the saddle horn, expecting shots to blister the afternoon air, but none did. A tree limb flashed over his head. Another tore at his shoulder. Straightening, he angled to the northeast and put a thorny thicket between him and his four pursuers. He had gone another thirty yards when a lusty oath and a strident whinny caused him to glance over a shoulder.

Kellim, the cowboy and the man in the flannel shirt had wisely given the thicket a wide berth, but not their companion in buckskins. He had foolishly plowed straight on through, or tried to, and the thorns were slashing the bay's legs and sides. The animal bucked and plunged in an anguished frenzy.

"Buxton, you damned lunkhead!" Kellim bawled, slowing. "What the hell were you thinking?"

Fargo didn't hear the man's response. He flew into a gully and up the other side, clods of dirt spewing from under the Ovaro's heavy hoofs. Dappled by the shadows of towering firs, he sped deeper into the forest. When next he checked, the cowboy and the man in the flannel shirt were still after him but they had lost a lot of ground. It gave him an idea.

Unfastening a rope from his saddle, Fargo loosened the noose. A couple of minutes later, after sweeping over a low rise, he veered toward a cluster of Sitka spruce. The two men were temporarily out of sight. They didn't see him bring the stallion to a stop, didn't see him quickly slip the noose over a limb at just the right height to suit his purpose. He swiftly threaded the other end through the noose and spurred the Ovaro a dozen yards to the right to another tree. Taking up the slack, he succeeded in looping the rope around another branch before the cowboy and the man in the flannel shirt came racing into view.

Riding ten feet farther, Fargo deliberately let them spot him, then reined around and resumed his flight.

The two men galloped after him, riding hell bent for leather. In their haste they failed to notice the rope. Riding abreast, they galloped between the two trees.

At the very last instant the cowboy awakened to the danger and tried to duck, but he was too close and the rope caught him across the shoulders, lifting him clear out of the saddle even as it did the same to the man in the flannel shirt. They were both hurled to the earth as if flung by invisible hands.

Reining the Ovaro around, Fargo drew his Colt and raced back. The man in flannel was on his side, moaning and clutching his neck; the rope had scraped upward, rubbing a large patch of skin raw, and blood was seeping between his fingers. The cowboy had fared better. Other than losing his high-crowned hat, he was only mildly stunned and was struggling to stand. He froze at the click of Fargo's Colt.

"Stay right where you are and keep your hands away from your hardware."

The two men glanced up. The cowboy shook his head to clear it, then grinned in wry appreciation. "I haven't had that trick pulled on me in a coon's age. I feel about as dumb as a stump and twice as useless." Curly blond hair spilled over his forehead, and he had a cleft jaw that matched the cleft in his upended hat. Up close, it was plain he was the youngest of the four, not much over eighteen, if that. Sitting back, he held his calloused hands out from his sides, making no attempt to resort to the Smith and Wesson. "You're sure a clever cuss."

The other man cursed furiously and rose on an elbow. He had sallow features pinched in pain. "Look at what you did to me, you bastard!" he fumed, pointing at the bloody smear. "You damned near took my head off!" His revolver had fallen from its holster and was well beyond his reach, but he looked as if he had half a mind to try for it anyway.

Fargo had no sympathy whatsoever. "You brought it on yourself." Warily sliding to the ground, he demanded, "Who hired you to dry gulch me?"

"All we were supposed to do was scare you off. Honest to God," the cowboy said. "And I have no idea who hired us. Kellim was the only one who ever met—"

"Shut up, Dakota!" the man in flannel barked. "We don't owe this buzzard any explanations."

Fire flared in Dakota's gray eyes. "The last hombre who used that tone on me, Yerrick, is pushing up weeds in an unmarked grave." Leaning to the right, he snagged his hat, brushed a few bits of grass off, and jammed it on his head. "You'd do well to remember that."

Yerrick sat up, his wound briefly forgotten. "Spare me, kid. I'm not a hick like Buxton. All that talk of you being fast on the draw doesn't impress me one bit."

"If you had any brains, it would," Dakota said.

Fargo was amused at how readily they had forgotten he was there. He jogged their memories by taking a step and wagging the Colt. "I take it the four of you haven't been partnered up very long?"

"Less than a week," Dakota answered, and was glared at by Yerrick. "Kellim offered forty dollars to each of us to camp out along the trail from the Columbia River and wait for a certain rider." He chuckled. "That would be you, hoss."

Fargo found it hard to dislike the young cowboy.

Yerrick, however, was another matter, and when be balled a fist and lunged at Dakota, Fargo took a step and slugged him with the Colt, smashing the barrel against his temple. Yerrick folded like a house of cards and lay twitching in an unconscious heap.

"I'm obliged," Dakota said. "But I can handle a puny polecat like him with both arms tied behind my back."

"Someone once told me that we're judged by the company we keep," Fargo commented. "If Yerrick is a polecat, what does that make you?"

"Broke," Dakota said, and sadly patted a pocket. "As busted as could be. And since I like to fill my belly as much as the next fella, I figured there wouldn't be any real harm in agreeing to help Kellim out. It wasn't as if he was hiring me to hurt somebody."

Fargo twirled the Colt into its holster. "Want some free advice? Pick a new line of work. You're not cut out to be an owlhoot." He turned toward the Ovaro.

Dakota blinked. "You're leaving? Just like that? Aren't you afraid I'll plug you as you're riding away?"

"You're not the kind," Fargo said. He prided himself on being a shrewd judge of character. Despite the cowboy's comment about an unmarked grave, Dakota wasn't a natural-born killer like some he had met.

Chuckling, the young man slapped his left chap. "Don't this beat all. You have every right to pistol-whip me senseless, yet you're treating me decent. Something tells me you'd do to ride the river with."

It was a compliment, and Fargo acknowledged it.

"What's an experienced cowhand like you doing in this neck of the woods? There aren't many cattle this far west."

"So I've noticed." Dakota frowned. "I'm from over Yankton way. About two months ago, I got me a hankering to see some of the country. I'd heard about the ocean, about how big it is and all those sea critters and such, and figured I'd have a look-see."

"With no money to your name?"

"I had pretty near a hundred dollars when I started," Dakota said proudly. "Never had that much to my name before. I figured it would last me six months or better." His grin blossomed. "I didn't count on a lucky galoot holding a full house to my three little queens."

Hooves drummed to the west. Kellim and Buxton were on their way.

Moving rapidly, Fargo untied his rope from the two trees and coiled it while hurrying to the Ovaro. "Washington Territory is no place for a cowman," he remarked. "If I were you, I'd head for Yankton first chance you get."

"I might just do that," Dakota said, and gave a little cough. "Listen, for what it's worth, I do know that the sidewinder who hired Kellim is a foreigner. From someplace like England or London or one of those countries."

"London is a city *in* England," Fargo set him straight, and forked leather.

"You don't say?" Dakota laughed. "I never had much book learning. I only got as far as the second grade and had to quit to help support my ma."

Kellim and Buxton were a lot nearer. Fargo touched his hat brim, saying, "Be seeing you," and trotted off. No one came after him, and over the course of the next half hour he worked his way back to the trail and continued northward. It was the main overland link between Seattle and Portland, and saw regular use. Scores of wagon wheels had dug ruts inches-deep into the soft soil, and hoofprints were everywhere.

In another mile, Fargo came on an isolated homestead consisting of a small cabin and a small garden perched on a bluff overlooking Puget Sound. A barechested man was chopping wood out front, and he nodded as Fargo went by.

From that point on, the water was almost always in sight. An unending succession of waves rolled shoreward where they broke on boulders or rippled across sandy beaches. Gulls wheeled and cawed, and out over the Sound pelicans dipped low to scoop fish into their big bills.

Fargo meandered down the widening trail and followed it to a dirt road. A moment later an elderly Indian stepped from the shadows under a nearby tree and started to cross in front of him. The Indian was dressed in a trade blanket wrapped tight around a bean-pole chest and spindly legs. On his head rested a circular cap of beaver fur. Head hung low, the old man blundered directly into the stallion's path.

"Watch out!" Fargo shouted, and hauled on the reins. The Ovaro shied and snorted, and a prancing hoof missed the old man by a cat's whisker. "You almost got trampled."

The Indian swivelled and glumly stared at him.

"What does it matter, white man?" he responded in fluent English. "My life will be as miserable in the next world as it is here."

"Why is that?" Fargo asked. He was trying to identify which tribe the man belonged to. Usually, he could tell by the style in which they wore their hair, since no two tribes wore it exactly alike. But the old man had done what many Pacific Northwest Indians who adopted to white ways had done and cut his hair short.

"My life has been ruined and there is nothing I can do," the man lamented. "My days are spent in misery, and will be forevermore."

"Why?" Fargo inquired. He thought liquor must be to blame. It was the bane of Indian existence, turning many a fine warrior into a sodden wreck. Among the Crows there was a saying that warriors who indulged in firewater ceased to be Crows.

"They have stolen it," the old man said and raised his arms to the heavens. "They have stolen it and will not give it back!"

Most whites wouldn't have given the Indian the time of day. Most would have assumed the old man was crazy and ridden on. But Fargo had lived among Indians, had learned many of the skills that kept him alive from his Sioux friends and others. "Stolen what?" he persisted, wondering now if the oldster had been robbed.

"My name," was the solemn reply.

"Who did such a thing?" Fargo asked, taking the man seriously. Among certain tribes a man's name was regarded as special, even sacred. The Apaches,

Excerpt from *PACIFIC POLECATS*

for instance, never told a white man their real name for fear it would give the whites power over them.

The Indian studied him. "You must be new here." Straightening, he said proudly, "I am Seathl. Perhaps you have heard of me?"

"Seathl?" Fargo repeated. It took a few seconds for the name to register. For him to recall the story he'd heard about how the new settlement was named after a local Indian chief who had befriended the early settlers. "You're the one they named Seattle after?"

"One and the same," Seathl confirmed. "Even though I asked them not to. Even though I *begged*."

"I don't savvy," Fargo admitted.

The lines on Seathl's face deepened. "They wanted to honor me. They wanted to show how grateful they were. And they laughed when I tried to tell them I would suffer."

"Suffer how?"

Seathl let out a heartfelt sigh. "Among my people a man's name must never be spoken. To do so brings him bad medicine. When the first whites came, I made the mistake of telling them my name. I should not have, but I had drunk much whiskey and my head was not right."

Fargo recollected a Chiricahua he once met, a famous warrior who became addicted to rotgut and ended his days groveling in the streets for money to feed his unquenchable thirst.

"The whites say my name all the time now, even though I have told them what it will do," Seathl said. "They have ears, but they do not use them. They have brains, but they do not think. To them, naming this

*163*

place after me was a sign of affection. To me, it means I will be tormented beyond the grave by endless troubles. Every time my name is spoken, something bad will happen."

"I am sorry," Fargo said. He'd learned long ago not to scoff at the beliefs of others. "I wish there was some way I could help." He couldn't very well ride up to the founding fathers and ask them to rename Seattle.

"There is," Seathl said, extending a palm. "Prove you are sincere. Five dollars will be enough. I ask more of most whites but you have not mocked me as most do."

"You go around asking everyone for money?"

"It is payment for the suffering to come," Seathl said in earnest. "If someone stole your horse but could not give it back, would you not make them pay for it? This is the same. My name has been stolen and can not be given back, so I ask for payment before I leave this world. Is that so wrong?"

There was a certain logic to the old's man reasoning. Fishing in a pocket, Fargo counted out five dollars. "Here you go."

Seathl clasped it to his chest, pivoted and bounded off into the gathering night with remarkable speed and agility for someone his age. "I thank you, white man!" his voice floated back. "I will drink a bottle in your memory."

"Son of a—" Fargo blurted. Shaking his head, he clucked to the Ovaro and went on his way.

Seattle was too new to have street lamps, and the streets were dark save for random shafts of lantern light cast from the windows he passed. It was the supper hour, and families were gathering indoors. He heard a baby bawling. A block away a mother screamed at her son to get his backside indoors or have it tanned. The mouthwatering aroma of cooked food wafted on the breeze, and Fargo's stomach growled, reminding him he hadn't eaten since dawn.

Most of the structures were log affairs. Given the supply of timber, that wasn't surprising. Toward the center of town, though, a number of frame buildings had been erected, among them a general store. It was open and Fargo was tempted to stop to replenish his provisions. But he had an appointment to keep.

At anchor in the bay were several tall-masted ships, their sails furled. Well beyond, lay the Olympic Peninsula. Stars were blossoming, among them the Big Dipper and the North Star. Deep in the woodland to the east, a wolf howled.

No town would be complete without its share of saloons and taverns. Seattle boasted seven watering holes. Given that the settlement's population only numbered in the low hundreds, it seemed like a lot until you considered there was little else to do once the sun sat. Mill workers, loggers and townsmen liked to gather for friendly drinks and sometimes not-so-friendly games of chance.

The establishment Fargo wanted was called the Cork and Keg. It was down by the water, and had the distinction of being frequented by Seattle's more prosperous residents. Drinks cost twice as much as everywhere else, but they were served in clean glasses by some of Seattle's prettiest fillies. Or so Fargo had been told by the man who had delivered the letter that brought him here.

Fargo drew rein at a hitch rail. It was nearly full and he had to shoulder a mare aside to make room for the Ovaro. "Behave yourself," he quipped, and climbed a short flight of steps. From within bubbled the hubbub of voices and coarse laughter. He opened the door and a cloud of cigar and cigarette smoke swirled out into the night.

Most of the tables were occupied and it was standing-room only at the bar. Judging by the tailor-made suits, expensive bowlers and ivory-handled canes in evidence, the fellow who told Fargo about the place hadn't exaggerated. No one else wore buckskins, and Fargo couldn't help feeling a bit conspicuous as he threaded through the card players and onlookers.

Suddenly, an immaculately dressed middle-aged man, wearing a short-brimmed hat slanted at a rakish angle, blocked his path. "I say! You're him, aren't you, Yank? You're the one we've been waiting for." His accent was unmistakably British.

Fargo looked him up and down. From a diamond stickpin to polished shoes, the man radiated oily charm. "And who might you be?"

Drawing himself up to his full height, the Englishman ran a manicured finger across a pencil-thin waxed mustache. "Why, I'm Reginald Thorndyke, at your service. I'm the one who sent for you."

"I was hoping you were," Fargo said, and punched him in the mouth.